Fission

Volume 1

An Anthology of Stories from the British Science Fiction Association

bsfa.co.uk

Edited By

Eugen Bacon and Gene Rowe

ISBN 978-1-910987-16-2

Contents

BSFA

The British Science Fiction Association

Fission #2 Volume 1.

First published in the UK in 2022 by the British Science Fiction Association (BSFA) & HWS Press.

Cover Design by Allen Stroud

ISBN: 978-1-910987-16-2

Foreword: Intergalactic Yammer Over a Cuppa

We're chalk and blue cheese, and that's okay.

If we were live-in partners, tomes would unlikely be the angst of our separation. Perhaps some tears or bother—if one party were to nobly offer the other a donation of one endeared volume.

Yeah, no.

Even then, some stories, like Aleksandra Hill's 'Words of Advice at the End of the World' and Ron Hardwick's 'Sage and the Resurrection of Doctor Chronos'—one on an apocalypse somewhere in America, the other on an alien visitation in Little Nibbling, somewhere on the Suffolk coast, each absurdist, witty and engorged with much-needed humour—hold such universal appeal, we were both ready to die for them.

Delightful fun was equally rampant in Phil Nicholls' sudden fiction 'Missy Hood Tweets'.

Alas, when we opened Fission #2 on 1 February to 15 March for original submissions in science fiction, we were not expecting 230-plus entries. Reading the lot was time-consuming and labour-intensive, but it was a labour of love.

Novel stories helped us disremember our calamitous world and reminisce about interactions with the 'other'—elusive techs as in Jeffrey Sommers' 'Free from Want'; deadly planets as in Tim O'Neal's 'Otherworldy Jellyfish'; and youth creating portals in Ellen Denton's 'The Portal'.

Napoleon showed up in Michael Noonan's time travel fiction 'All the Time in the World' and Caroline Misner's ingenious misnomer 'The Epsilon Requirement'.

We discovered rogue climates and rampant plagues.

We saw distinctive cameos or full-blown appearances of AI goldmines as in Clare Turner's 'In Person' and David

Tallerman's 'Face the Inevitable'. Cybernetics too, in KC Grifant's 'Cynscout'; nanotechnology in Peter Medeiros' 'Bad Architecture'... And body doubles in Maddison Stoff's 'Zombie Harold Holt Returns to Parliament' and Ian Whates' 'The FenZone'.

The immense diversity of speculative fiction empowered a Latin spell class in Mary Soon Lee's charmer 'Truth Conquers All' and two mesmeric black speculative fiction tales in Chinaza Eziaghighala's 'Osimiri' and Andrew Darlington's 'Buffalo Soldiers'.

Indeed, we very much enjoyed reading the stories and it was unquestionable we would publish two volumes. We were thrilled to accept 17 ingenious stories for Fission #2 Vol.1, together with a translation—Patricia Garcia-Rojo's 'The Fifth Awakening' that's part of our tremendous partnership with the Spanish publication CELSIUS.

Huge thanks to Allen Stroud, who engineered this arrangement, and for tackling the pioneer flagship Fission #1 on top of lecturing, writing, the pandemic, and all the demands of his BSFA Chair role. Allen, you're ace.

This staggering volume of Fission #2 teasers is a promise of more titillating enchanters in Vol. 2, out in November 2022. Until then, enjoy a degustation of unforgettable science fiction at a dire time when the universe needs literary escapade more than ever.

Stay safe and healthy!

Yours truly,
Eugen Bacon & Gene Rowe
Fission Editors

Sage and the Resurrection of Doctor Chronos

Ron Hardwick

The doorbell rang one fine day in mid-May, back in 2017. I live in a one-roomed apartment in the village of Little Nibbling, on the Suffolk coast. It's a quiet place, where the main excitement for the inhabitants is watching the leaves cascade down from the trees in autumn.

My name is Alvin Rivers and I'm a freelance historian, dealing exclusively in the history of Suffolk. My speciality is the Bronze Age. I write for a variety of publications and, because my parents left me comfortably off when they died, I have no need to obtain a proper job.

I opened the front door.

A remarkable apparition stood before me. It took the form of a most attractive woman, but whose dress was, quite frankly, a little bizarre. She was clad in an orange and green diagonally striped jump-suit with a high collar, constructed from a material I didn't recognise, but which strongly resembled kitchen foil. A blue bandana of similar material wound round her head like a coiled cobra. Her hair was long, and a peculiar shade of vermilion, but her most arresting feature was her eyes. They were as dark and deep as oil wells and they seemed to bore through me like gimlets. Her skin was of a golden hue but that might have been a trick of the light.

She looked me up and down with those impenetrable eyes for several seconds, before speaking.

'You're a bit weedy, but I suppose you'll have to do.'

I have to admit that I'm no Charles Atlas, but I took exception to the 'weedy' part.

'Madam,' I said, in a frosty manner, 'I don't think I've had the pleasure.'

'Nor will you ever have.'

'What I mean is, I don't think we've been properly introduced.'

'My name is Sage. I take it you are Rivers, the expert on the history and anthropology of all things Suffolk?'

'I am Alvin Rivers, yes, but I hesitate to say I am an expert on *all* things Suffolk.'

'Well, Rivers,' said Sage, 'I am in sore need of your help.'

'Would you care to step inside?' I asked her. 'It is unseemly to be discussing matters on the doorstep. My neighbours have the annoying tendency to peep through their curtains and take note of everything that occurs within their purview.'

'Oh, you don't need to worry about them,' said Sage.

'Why ever not?'

'For the simple reason I've blanked all their minds. They will remember nothing that they've witnessed over the last thirty minutes.'

I looked at this woman standing on my doorstep, hostile as a cornered wasp, yet ravishingly pretty with her high sculpted cheekbones, full lips and piercing eyes, and wondered whether my invitation to entertain her inside was wise. After all, you get so many nutcases about these days. Sage seemed to read my thoughts.

'You are perfectly safe with me. I'll cause you no harm. I *will* enter your miserable abode to continue our discourse.'

She strode languidly into my small living room and sat in my one easy chair.

'Cup of tea?' I asked.

'I have no need of your earthly beverages, thank you.'

'You don't mind if I make one for myself? I haven't had my breakfast yet.'

'Go ahead.'

I busied myself in the kitchen and brought back a mug of tea and a slice of toast.

'Now, to business,' said Sage. 'Doubtless you wish to know why I need the help of a man as insignificant as yourself?'

'I was wondering, yes.'

'I am obliged to inform you I am not of your world.'

'You don't say.'

'I was born on the planet Tennuria, on the other side of Jupiter and up to now regarded simply as one of its moons. Astronomers here are so crude and unintelligent. My parents sent me here when I was nineteen of your years old, to learn Earth ways and because my home world was, and now is again, riven by a fatal disease.'

'Of course,' I said, humouring this madwoman, 'I can see you had no other choice but to come from the planet Tennuria to Little Nibbling.'

Sage didn't seem to understand irony because she ignored my remark.

'My parents are now deceased.'

'I'm sorry to hear about your parents. My own...'

'We have no time to discuss details pertaining to your life. We must act before it is too late.'

'Too late for what?' I asked.

'We thought an ancient disease that has dogged us for millennia had died out, but a few weeks ago it reappeared in its most virulent form. There are several million people who inhabit our home world, but this rampant disease, which causes our internal organs to fuse together, leading to an agonising death, is reducing those numbers by thousands every day. We have just one chance of reversing the situation.'

'Just one chance? What is that?' I asked.

'I have to find, and resurrect, the corpse of Doctor Chronos, who is buried in Suffolk, but I know not where. Because I am the only Tenurian at present domiciled in England, only I can save my people.'

'Who is this Doctor Chronos?'

'He came to Earth during the period your Earthlings refer to as the Bronze Age. We know that he took the formula for arresting this disease with him. There was a missing ingredient in the formula that could only be found on Earth.'

'He was alone?'

'No. He took with him an assistant, one Spithrax, who returned to Tennuria after the Doctor's demise to advise the Elders that Chronos had died. Spithrax's text talks of a miracle cure to this fatal disease in the hands of Doctor Chronos. That is how we are aware that a cure exists and Chronos holds the key to its elimination.'

'How do you know he's interred in Suffolk?' I asked.

'Spithrax's text also describes the doctor's last resting place as 'a land flat and green, with nary a hill in sight, criss-crossed with innumerable streams, ruled by a tribe that call themselves Iceni. The text therefore clearly indicates that the grave is here in Suffolk.'

'Look, Sage, if that is indeed your name. I'm having great difficulty in believing anything you say. You show up at nine in the morning, dressed like a merchandiser promoting *Sanilav* lavatory cleaner, claiming to be from a distant planet, and you want me to help you find a medic who's been dead since the third century B.C. It's a little bit fanciful, don't you think?'

She rose from her seat, walked over to me, held her face inches from mine and looked at me with those dagger-like eyes. Everything went blank and I started to sway at the knees. She caught me before I fell, and stood me upright again. Then, in seconds, I saw things as clearly as if they were etched on glass.

'Now do you believe me?'

I nodded.

'I have knowledge in my brain far greater than you can ever conceive,' said Sage. 'I can transmit my thoughts to you by means of a technique we call tele-hypnokinetics, and I can blank minds of people within a radius of two miles for a period of up to thirty minutes. But I cannot reverse the process and transfer all your thoughts, ideas, experience and beliefs into my superior brain.'

'Why not?'

'The Elders on Tennuria felt that would afford me too much power. The special gifts that I alone have are only granted to a Tennurian child once every thousand years. I was the fortunate, or perhaps unfortunate, one.'

'Unfortunate?'

'You have no idea what a burden it is to possess these powers. For example, I could hypnotise you and command you to transfer all your worldly belongings to me.'

'You'd get slim pickings there,' I said.

'I could do it with the richest man in the world, not a microbe like you, and that would grant me powers beyond comprehension. I could use my tele-hypnokinetics to force politicians to start wars, if I had a mind to. Now do you see what a burden it is to stay on the right side of good and evil?'

'I do. I'm sorry I doubted you.'

I changed the subject.

'How did the good doctor and your parents travel to Earth from Tennuria?'

'We are an advanced people. We have built inter-galactic space podules for thousands of years. These travel at the speed of light. We have also mastered the science of placing a body in stasis and timing its re-awakening to coincide with entry to a destination planet's atmosphere.'

'Remarkable,' I said.

'It is nothing to a Tennurian.'

'So your main purpose in collaring me is to help you find out where your precious Doctor Chronos is buried?'

'Yes. As I have said, I do not have access to all the knowledge in the world but, I daresay, if the Elders had allowed it, I could have readily taken all that information in hand. I will have to rely on you, Rivers, to help me locate his burial chamber.'

'How on earth do you intend to revive a two-thousand-year-old skeleton?' I asked.

'With this.'

Sage produced a golden bracelet from the pocket of her metallic jump-suit.

'When we find him, he'll be wearing a similar bracelet on one of his skeletal wrists. We will merely have to place this on his other wrist and the hypo-telekinetic energy that will be released will revive him as surely as I revived you.'

'Why can't you carry out that procedure on the people who are dying on your planet?' I asked.

'Because there are no other examples of this bracelet in existence. This one is over two thousand of your Earth years old. Doctor Chronos will be wearing the only other example.'

I nodded and reached up to my map shelf to withdraw a chart which showed the sites of Bronze Age burial grounds in the county. I spread it out on the dining room table.

'How many burial sites are there?' asked Sage.

'At least nine, but more may exist.'

'Is there any way we can narrow down that number?'

'I think so. The largest is near Wattisham. Twenty-one skeletons have been unearthed there. It's a large site, and more skeletons are believed to lie undiscovered further to the east. I would start there.'

I had a sudden thought.

'Hang on, what if your doctor friend was one of those already dug up?'

'That is unlikely.'

'Why?'

'The skeletons of Tennurians remain a vivid shade of purple, regardless of the length of time they lie under the soil. I think that might have been remarked upon if Chronos' skeleton had been uncovered, even by such a collection of singularly obtuse archaeologists and journalists that currently reside in England.'

'Well, if that's the case, I would start at Wattisham. I warn you, though, the site is on private land and the landowner, Lord Scrivener-Sachs of Wattisham, does not take kindly to trespassers. He is known to wander about with a twelve-bore shotgun under his arm and to let fly at anyone he sees skulking about his property.'

'I do not skulk around anyone's property,' said Sage, loftily, 'and I shall deal with his Lordship as and when the need arises.'

'I'm just giving you the lie of the land,' I said.

'You have transport?' asked Sage.

'I own a car,' I said. 'A Morris Traveller.'

'Good, I had to get the omnibus here,' said Sage. 'Most uncomfortable.'

'Even though you have conquered the science of space travel?'

'My space podule is not geared for travel along the A12.'

* * *

We found the site without difficulty. I parked in a lay-by and we crossed a field to reach the burial grounds. A plethora of notices warning trespassers of the dire consequences should they be unlucky enough to be caught, festooned the barbed wire fence over which we were obliged to climb.

'We don't need to climb anything,' said Sage. 'My suit is indestructible. All I need to do is barge through the fence. You can follow.'

Sure enough, Sage pressed hard against the wire with her body until a wooden post snapped at its base and we stepped over the grounded wire.

'How will we find the exact location of the remains of Doctor Chronos?' I asked. 'This site has a diameter of quarter of a mile, he'll be twenty feet underground and we didn't bring a shovel.'

'Buffoon,' said Sage. 'Do you think I came unprepared?'

From her tunic she withdrew a metal artefact that looked something like a water diviner. Within seconds it started to beep and the ends glowed red. She walked in each direction until the machine's bleep became a screech, and then she continued a further hundred yards or so till the diviner screamed like a jet engine at full throttle.

'There,' she said. 'Down there.'

'Why couldn't you have pointed that thing from where your, what did you call it, space podule, landed?' I asked.

'The refulgirator only has a range of about half a mile. I needed you to help me identify the site before I could use it.'

A bellicose voice, harsh and forbidding, drifted across the field to us.

'You there, get off my land or I'll fill you full of shot.'

A ruddy-faced gentleman with a handlebar moustache, a deer-stalker, an evil-looking shotgun and an equally evil-looking mastiff came lumbering across to where we were standing.

'Get them, Rufus.'

The hound, jaws slavering with the anticipation of a mouthful of my flesh, bounded towards us. Sage turned to face it while I stood cowering behind her. There appeared to be a pencil-line of concentrated green light coming from her eyes towards the dog. It stopped as if it had collided with a brick wall and started to whimper.

The gentleman drew alongside her.

Sage favoured him with her steely gaze and, in seconds, Lord Scrivener-Sachs of Wattisham lay senseless on his face in the grass.

'We shan't have any bother from either of them,' said Sage, 'at least for half an hour.'

She took a small cylinder from her top pocket (her jump-suit contained about a dozen pockets—now I could see why).

'What's that?' I asked.

'It's a Tennurian skeleton-seeking explosive device. It will measure the precise distance from here to Doctor Chronos and it will burrow down and place itself in the right spot to ensure the crater is correctly excavated. It will then explode and will reveal Chronos' remains. If I were you, I would stand back, unless you want a face full of soil.'

Sage placed the cylinder on the grass, whereupon a digging arm appeared from its carcass and started its excavations with the speed of a racing motorcycle. I dragged the inert form of his Lordship back a hundred yards, and the now servile hound meekly followed Sage the same distance.

The mighty explosion occurred within a minute, and sent a column of grass, soil, clay and stones 50 feet into the air. It was a remarkably localised explosion, for it uncovered a crater only 12 feet by 6.

Sage and I walked to the edge and looked down. Staring back at us through sightless eyes was a purple skeleton with a bracelet on its left wrist. Its arms were folded comfortably across its chest.

'How come the Iceni didn't steal the bracelet?' I asked.

'They had no opportunity. Presumably, they were terrified of Chronos and would go nowhere near him.'

'They could have robbed his dead body.'

'He made his own grave.'

'What do you mean?'

Sage turned round to look at me.

'We Tennurians know when our demise is imminent. We receive a verbal communication from the Elders. We have a short time to prepare for our own burial. Spithax would have helped the Doctor dig his own grave and would have covered the corpse with soil once Chronos passed on.'

The explosion avoided creating steep and impassable sides to Chronos' grave, but ensured a gradual slope on one side, down to the skeleton. Sage slid on her behind to where Chronos lay, and, in a matter of seconds, had fastened the bracelet on his other wrist.

I watched in amazement as the skeleton rose, stood and shook itself like a terrier emerging from a river. My eyes almost popped out of my head as flesh and skin started to adorn Chronos' skeletal remains and, when he was again fully formed, his body was clothed with the same jump-suit as Sage's.

The pair climbed slowly up the incline and I pulled first Sage, then Chronos up the final couple of feet and out of the crater. Chronos, unaccustomed to the light, blinked rapidly until he became accustomed to it.

Sage placed the flat of her hand against the large forehead of the doctor and held it there for 30 seconds or so.

'He now knows the English language,' she said. 'He could only speak in the obscure Germanic language used by the Iceni.'

'So you found me,' said Chronos. 'I wondered how long it would take.'

'Nearly three thousand years,' I said.

'Who is this?' asked Chronos.

'This is Rivers. In a small way, he has helped me to locate you.'

'Excuse me, I prefer to be called Alvin, and I helped you a lot more than you've given me credit for.'

'He's English,' said Sage. 'They tend towards self-aggrandisement.'

'Here, I object to that,' I said.

'We should leave,' said Sage, ignoring me. 'Lord Whatever-His-Name-Is of Wattisham will wake shortly and his finger is too itchy on the trigger of his weapon to make our remaining here safe.'

Chronos nodded and we made our way back to the car.

'What form of chariot is this?' asked Chronos.

'A car. A genuine classic. A Morris Traveller,' I said.

'It travels at the speed of light, like our space podules?'

'Not exactly, but it will do sixty flat out if the wind is behind us.'

'Climb in,' said Sage. 'We will repair to Rivers' home.'

* * *

We were seated silently round my dining room table when Sage spoke.

'Doctor, you must return as soon as possible to Tennuria. You must eradicate the disease.'

The doctor nodded.

'You can use my space podule. It is hidden a few miles west of here. Rivers will drive us.'

'Hang on,' I said. 'You told me that the doctor still needs one ingredient to complete the antidote. It could only be found on Earth. He can't leave without it. Doctor Chronos, what is it?'

'It is a plant, common on Earth,' said Chronos. 'It has a remarkable fragrance, and its oil is what I need to complete the antidote. Only a minute drop of oil for each injection is necessary. I require several rooted specimens of this plant in order to germinate many more under laboratory conditions on Tennuria.'

'What's it called?' I asked.

'I have no idea what you English call it, but we Temmurians know it as Ioclexorn.'

'Ioclexorn?'

'It is written of in the ancient texts,' said Sage. 'We used to grow the plant on Tennuria, but the genus died out with the great drought which occurred in the Aeon of Turmoil.'

'That doesn't help an awful lot,' I said. 'Hold on, I do have a book of British plants somewhere. It's full of illustrations. I'll fetch it.'

It was a large hard-backed volume and I laid it on the table. Chronos flipped over each page and studied the flora intently. Halfway through, he stabbed his finger excitedly at the page.

'That is the plant.'

I looked over his shoulder.

'Lavender,' I said.

'Where can we find this lavender?' asked Sage.

'There's a garden centre near Woodbridge,' I said. 'A few miles away. I'll go. I'm not sure whether they'd serve either of you. You can stay here in the meantime.'

* * *

I bought two dozen plants.

'That is acceptable,' said Chronos. 'Now you must take me to the space podule.'

The three of us set off in the Morris. The podule was hidden under a pile of straw in an abandoned barn on a derelict farm near Bilderton.

'Why not use your own podule?' I asked Chronos.

'Battery's flat,' he said.

'They only hold their charge for forty years,' added Sage.

'How will Sage get home, then?' I asked. 'This thing's about the size of an Isetta bubble-car. You'll never get two people in there.'

Chronos and Sage exchanged meaningful glances.

'Never you mind,' said Sage.

We stood at the barn entrance while Chronos started the podule, the lavender plants perched precariously on the main console.

He waved and, in a blink, he was gone and all that was left was a shimmering light and flattened straw where the podule had stood.

We left the barn and headed back to the car.

Suddenly, Sage turned away and seemed to be talking to her wrist. She didn't speak in English, but in what seemed to be a series of clicks and sibilant whistles.

She was in a serious mood when she returned to the Morris.

'Sage, what's wrong?'

She smiled at me but didn't reply. Instead, she held a finger to my lips.

We drove home in silence.

I stopped the car outside my flat. Sage stayed where she was.

'Alvin?'

I was shocked to hear her use my Christian name.

'Sage?'

'Will you help me?'

'If I can.'

'You saw me speaking into a communicator?'

'Oh, is that what it was?'

'The Elders on Tennuria have communicated with me.'

'Oh, yes?' I didn't like the sound of this.

'It's time.'

'Time?'

She nodded. 'I told you all this was pre-ordained and that they would communicate with me when it was my time. Well, that time is now.'

'I won't allow it,' I said. 'They've no jurisdiction over you here on Earth. You can stay here with me. I'll take you to see Doctor Truelove, my GP. He'll be able to find something to help you.'

She shook her head sadly.

'My body is, what do you English say?—hard-wired? — to fail at a specific point in time. In my case, my demise has been delayed until my job here is finished. Now that Chronos is on his way back to Tennuria with the antidote, my task here is fulfilled. I have but two hours left to live.'

'Two hours?'

'Yes. You must take me back to the burial site and make sure my corpse is properly covered. You possess a digging implement?'

'I have a spade, yes, for clearing snow.'

'Then fetch it, please, and take me back.'

Shocked to the core, I did as I was bid. We were back at the site within the hour. Of Lord Scrivener-Sachs of Wattisham or the Hound of the Baskervilles, there was no sign.

'Not there,' said Sage. 'A new grave, just to the right of Chronos'.'

I dug a shallow grave, 3 feet deep.

'I grow weak,' she said when I returned to the surface, and she leaned heavily on my shoulder.

'Take this cylinder and place it on top of the mound of soil. Press that tiny button on the side to activate it after you have laid me to rest. The subsequent explosion will replace the soil exactly as it was. Now help me down.'

I slithered down to the graveside with Sage in my arms. She was as light as a pillow.

'Lay me down gently, please, Alvin,' she said, 'so I can rest easy.'

I did so. She looked up at me with those dark rapier eyes.

'You are a good man, Alvin,' she said. 'You have helped Chronos and I to save a whole race of people. The Doctor will make sure you are mentioned in our texts—a hero from Little Nibbling in the County of Suffolk, England. May your God look after you and protect you until the day you die.'

She closed her eyes and gradually her breathing became shallower until it ceased altogether.

Blinded by tears, I folded her arms across her chest and stood silently by her side for several minutes. Fearing the return of the noble Lord and his mutt, I scrambled up the slope to the surface, placed the cylinder where Sage had instructed me, pressed the button and ran quickly for cover.

There was another huge explosion and Sage was entombed forever.

Miraculously, the soil was once again covered with grass, and you couldn't tell where she was buried. I kept my eyes firmly on the spot under which she lay, and I pressed a twig into the ground to remind me, until I could return with something more permanent.

I went back to the car, fashioned a cross from two pieces of wood, lashed them together with string, and replaced the twig with my primitive cross.

I return each week to her grave.

I always place a sprig of lavender on the spot under which she lies sleeping. I think she would appreciate the fact that someone she scarcely knew cares so deeply for her.

Words of Advice at the End of the World

Aleksandra Hill

Asked and Answered is a weekly advice column brought to you by Constance Sienkiewicz at Gneiss News. Have a question? Email her at constance@gneissnews.com.

September 7, 20X3

Q. Rude realists: My spouse and I are realists and we're raising our children (3, 5, 9) to be realists, too. We've never sheltered them from the truth or indoctrinated them with lies (not even 'harmless' ones like Santa Claus).

A few weeks ago, our eldest ('Lorrie') was watching the news with us when JPL *[Ed. Note: Jet Propulsion Labs, which manages NASA's Center for Near-Earth Object Studies]* released its first report. Since then, she's been fascinated with learning about apocalyptic scenarios—not just the asteroid that killed the dinosaurs, but also Chernobyl and nuclear winter, pandemics, etc. Aside from a couple of nightmares, she's taken her learning in stride and we're proud of how inquisitive and self-directed she is. We want her to be prepared for the real world.

The problem is a birthday party that Lorrie attended last weekend. We dropped her off for a sleep-over and, just a few hours later, the birthday girl's parents asked that we pick Lorrie up! She had apparently 'upset' the other girls in attendance by talking about everything she's learned 'in extreme detail.' The amended numbers had just come out that morning citing an 80% chance of collision, so I understand that tension was high—but they also insinuated that we're bad parents and it's not 'appropriate' for Lorrie to be learning at her advanced level. I disagreed vehemently and noted that there's no reason to panic yet; the numbers had been jumping between 50% and 75% for the last few weeks, after all.

Since then, Lorrie's friends have cancelled playdates. Worse, we weren't invited to a neighbourhood meeting on impact preparations. When I found out after the fact and asked the head of the homeowners association, she said she'd heard we're 'not concerned about the situation' in an impossibly snide tone. I'm at a loss about what to do.

A: Even if—and that's a big if—a nine-year-old is mature enough to cope with the horror of what nuclear radiation does to a human body(!) and what a global extinction could look like, that doesn't mean her classmates are. Have you talked to Lorrie about what's appropriate to share with friends, or—as I suspect—are your children the ones telling everyone else how stupid they are for believing in Santa?

Furthermore, a 20% chance of mass death in less than two months on a *global scale* isn't something to wave off. The fear is real. I'm a grown woman and I'm terrified for myself, my parents, my friends! I hope we can all laugh about how worried we were in a month or two.

But we don't know what the future holds, so you should apologise to your neighbours for being an ass. More importantly, remember that there might not be a world for your daughter to be prepared for in a few weeks' time. Let her be a kid.

* * *

September 14, 20X3

Q: I realised long ago that I was never the marrying kind—a perma-bachelor, if you will. My girlfriend of eight years knew that when we started dating. But when the report came out, things got (unsurprisingly) hysterical. She started packing up, saying that she'd rather spend her last days with her parents than with someone who doesn't appreciate her. I realised that there was nobody else in the world I wanted to spend the rest of my life with, and we decided to get married at the end of September, just after she's due.

I was the happiest man in the world until last night, when they announced that the numbers were wrong and there likely won't be a collision. I realised I'd deluded myself about marriage in the panic. I don't know how to let her down easy. She's already told all her family and friends.

What do I do?

A: Most of the letters I've received this week have been updates—families reunited and friendships mended after the initial report, thrilled that they have more time together. I've been calling my parents daily, just revelling in the fact that I can see them at Christmas.

The majority of the rest were people who'd told asshole bosses to stuff it and now need to figure out how to get their jobs back. (Answer: life's too short for an asshole boss, even without the threat of global cataclysm. Take this as an opportunity to find a new job.)

And then there's you.

Please leave her. You don't want to be with her and she's better off without you.

* * *

September 21, 20X3

Q: My wife and I both work long hours. We have a weekly date night to make sure that we're making time for each other between taking kids, deadlines, and business trips. For the last few months, we've started each one with a randomly drawn 'What if' statement from a card deck my wife got us for Christmas. They've led to spirited debates about what superpowers we'd pick as a crime-fighting duo and what 10 books we'd want to have on a deserted island (she nixed 'How to Build a Boat' as no fun).

Everything was great until last week, when the question was about surviving a zombie apocalypse. I said that I'd just get bit on Day 1—I enjoy *The Walking Dead* as much as anyone, but I'm not cut out to live through a horror movie!

My wife got really upset, asking if that counted for the asteroid as well. She ran upstairs in tears when I didn't answer fast enough and now she won't speak to me. What do I do?

A: I don't know what faith you married in, or if you married in any, but you might be familiar with the phrase 'Till death us do part.' Most people don't assume that their spouse will hasten their demise; that might feel like a broken promise, *especially* when children are involved.

You didn't mention if this occurred before the announcement that the report of an erroneous calculation was itself an error, so it's hard to say just how callous you were. Given the probability of impact is now 90%, maybe your wife set up drawing that card because she didn't know how else to bring up the subject.

You haven't mentioned your gender, but are you the stronger or more protective of the two of you? If so, did she have expectations for her own safety based on that? Either way, it seems like she thought that it was both of you versus the world, and now she's coming to learn that she's going to be alone if the going gets really tough. We're already seeing the beginnings, with food stockpiling and impossibly high gas and travel prices.

You should start off by apologising, then ask what she's thinking. Are there friends or family nearby with whom she can shelter if you're dead? People who will take her in and not kick her out—or, worse, hurt her—at the first sign of shortage or illness? If you're dead set on not sticking around (apologies for the phrasing), the least you can do is help now.

* * *

September 28, 20X3

Q: My wife and I hit a rough patch last year. She lost her job; I was working long hours with a lot of stress. Our children had a variety of issues from then-undiagnosed ADHD to a run-in with the law. Eventually, things improved and now we're doing better than ever.

There's just one snag. During that time, I had a dalliance with another employee at my company. I know what you're thinking! But my wife and I married young enough that I didn't get to date or explore. I thought I was okay with that until my marriage felt like it was crumbling; then, I thought it was too late—until 'Theodore'.

Constance, we love each other. He knows about my family, knows what our relationship is, and that's never been a problem till now. It's still not a *problem,* except he doesn't have any living family and moved across the country for this job less than a year ago. He's got no-one but me.

My wife and I had a nuclear shelter built on our property during the Ozyorsk nuclear scare. We agreed to keep it under wraps so people don't try to force their way in if the worst happens. If it happens, I want Theodore to be there. We have enough food and space for him, and he has nowhere else to go.

What do I do? If I tell my wife about my infidelity, it'll break her heart and she might reject Theodore—and me. If I ask for him to stay as a friend, she might not agree or suggest others stay with us, which risks the secrecy and longevity of our shelter.

Or it might all come out while we're sheltering. But I imagine him alone as the sky turns to fire and I can't bear that, either.

A: Listen: as of this afternoon, impact is 100% certain. None of these problems matter because we're all going to die in 18 days. Tell your wife, don't tell your wife, it's going to have the same result. We'll be reduced to smithereens or end up choking on an atmosphere filled with ash or freezing to death or starving.

If you're not sure about all the ways our lives might end, tune into your local news station, where all they're fucking showing is the ways a meteor can kill us. I would give anything to see my parents again before the end, but I can't even get to New York—not with prices the way they are. I am completely alone, just like Theodore will be.

On the off chance that you make it and Theodore doesn't, will you be able to live with that guilt? You might as well take the risk.

Update: I wanted to give you the latest on my letter (*Ed. Note: September 14, 'Perma-Bachelor'*). I did as you suggested and left my fiancée. She spent most of what was left of our money after the markets crashed on a plane ticket to her parents' place. Our friends won't speak to me anymore and she blocked my number. I don't even know if she gave birth.

The world is ending and I've got nobody. Thanks for nothing.

A: Good. I hope you die alone.

* * *

September 29, 20X3
Dear readers,

I want to apologise for yesterday. Thank you to everyone who reached out. The news... I didn't take it well. I'd been living with worry for my parents' safety and the knowledge that I couldn't afford to make it up to New York with gas prices the way they are. I was scared to hitchhike with all the stories going around about theft and abandonment. I was tired of helping strangers when no-one's helping me.

And then a former letter-writer (*Ed* Note: September 7, 'Disastrous Date Night'*) reached out, saying she and her wife are heading up to New York and I can hitch a ride with her family. I'm writing this from the back of a minivan, not quite able to believe my fortune.

You may have noticed that Gneiss News has stopped updating since most of the staff quit. Don't worry: I'm going to keep answering as many emails as I can. Quite frankly, it's the only thing keeping me sane. And send me your updates! (Good vibes only, please.)

Lastly, to our first letter writer from yesterday: I'm sorry for how callously I treated your question, but my answer is unchanged. Our chances are so small now, why not take a risk on extending kindness? On the chance that things work out... we need all the hope we can get.

To the writer of the update: please continue to go fuck yourself.

Love,

Connie

**It's me. I'm Editor now.*

* * *

October 10, 20X3

Update: I think my ex is the person who wrote in about being a 'perennial bachelor.'

Constance, I wasted almost a decade with that man, always convincing myself it 'wasn't that bad.' I brought a child into this world who probably won't see the first month of his life. We left Boston for our friends' cottage, but it isn't much in the way of shelter and it's hard not to despair. I can't do much except wait for the end of the world.

By all accounts, this is a horrible end.

But… I want to thank you for your advice. The last couple of weeks—the ones without him—have also been some of the happiest, freest that I can remember. Seeing my parents with their first and only grandchild has been a treasure. Thank you for giving me that.

A: Good luck out there. For anyone still reading this and waiting for a sign: this is it.

* * *

October 12, 20X3

Update: I'm the letter-writer with the secret lover who… isn't a secret anymore. We're all heading to the shelter now. My kids get along great with Theodore, but they don't know the whole story. My wife… we talked until dawn, the night I told her.

The first thing she said was to remind us of our wedding vows. The ones where we'd promised to love, honour, cherish until the Earth stopped spinning.

It was the first time in my life I'd ever been early to anything, she said, and then she laughed, and then she cried, and then I cried, and then we couldn't stop.

I don't know if she'll forgive me if we survive this. But I do know that her generosity will make this apocalypse one *worth* surviving. She ran the numbers: we could make it 3 months with 12 people in the shelter, and isn't that something? And so it's the kids, and her, and me, and Theodore and *his* two friends, and our son's best friend's family and our daughter's roommates. It's going to be a tight fit, but you were right.

We need all the hope we can get.

A: You won't see this, but I'm wishing you all the best.

* * *

October 14, 20X3

Dear readers,

I'm writing this from a sheltering facility in Brooklyn, packed cheek-to-jowl with my parents and hundreds of strangers as they process us to get underground. It's two days before impact and this is the last instalment of the column, hopefully for now, probably forever.

Where I used to get a few dozen emails a week, I received hundreds—sometimes over a thousand—almost every day for most of the last 6 weeks. In that time, you've fallen in love, you've broken hearts, you've grown your families and lost loved ones. You lied, cheated, surprised, triumphed. You've made mistakes.

We've made so many mistakes.

Whatever has happened: now's the time to do our best. Love each other. Be good to each other. If you have shelter, fill it as best you can—with friends, family, acquaintances.

I don't know what I'd advise in normal times. But right now, the answer seems astoundingly clear: choose love.

See you on the other side, maybe.

Constance Sienkiewicz

Face the Inevitable

David Tallerman

Schmidt rose just before 10, slipped a gown around his thin frame, and went downstairs. He started the kettle and, while it was boiling, went into the main room to stare out through a gap in the curtains.

With the right angle, Schmidt could see the main gate, and between its bars the protestors beyond. He couldn't read their signs and banners, nor could he hear what they were chanting through the thickened security glass, though the sound was a faint susurrus. There was a camera embedded above the gate, from which he could have called up footage had he wanted to, but it had only ever been used by the police, after the last attempted break-in. It had been a long time, too, since the protestors had anything new to say, and Schmidt's interest in them was purely habit.

When the kettle summoned him with its shrill artificial whistle, Schmidt went back into the kitchen and made coffee, that being one of the few luxuries he allowed himself. And, as often happened, the coffee and the memory of the protestors came together to spark another recollection—that of the beginning.

Every time, he thought how ridiculous it was to suppose there'd been one occasion deserving of that title, *beginning*. Every time, he was forced to admit it didn't matter. He couldn't erase the memory, nor convince himself that its significance was other than what he'd come to believe. All he could do was remember as he always had.

* * *

'What you can't admit,' Kahn said, 'is that there has to be *something*. I won't call it soul, spirit... I don't want you bellowing at me! But there's an element, inimitably human, that we'll never be able to define.'

'You're right,' Schmidt replied. 'You're absolutely right.' He took a sip from his thimble of a cup. 'I *can't* admit it.'

They were drinking coffee, proper coffee, in one of Los Angeles' last three independent outlets. They'd had to book days ahead to get a table, but the coffee was worth it: thick and black, it tasted as if it had been drawn from deep within the earth.

So as not to ruin his enjoyment, Schmidt tried to subdue his irritation that Kahn, who'd devoted her life to scrutinising the intricacies of the human brain, was spouting such nonsense. But he didn't try terribly hard.

'You'd think these days, with the million and one insights we have into the mind, that you of all people would know better than to throw around the "s" word.'

'Soul?' said Kahn, mocking a little. 'That's the word you mean, yes?'

Schmidt felt inexplicably provoked. 'Perhaps a predisposition is blunting your judgement,' he proposed. 'Is your family religious?'

'I'm an atheist, and so is my father. Just as we're both psychiatrists. All right, I shouldn't have said "soul", but that doesn't change my point. There's a hole at the centre of us no science will probe, and you'd do well to admit it.'

'I won't,' Schmidt insisted. 'And *you'd* do well to stop trying to make me.'

She smiled, still ironical. 'Or what? You'll prove me wrong?'

'Maybe I will,' he said. 'For spoiling my coffee. Maybe that's precisely what I'll do.'

* * *

Schmidt took his drink outside. He went through the back door so the protestors wouldn't see. He avoided the front of the house altogether, and since he refused to employ staff—even assuming anyone would work for him—the garden had become a jungle. One day, he hoped, its untamed escalation would hide the gates from view.

Schmidt walked across the patio, avoiding the edge of the dried-up pool, and along a path of white gravel to the rear entrance of his compound, a metal door sunk into the stuccoed wall. Beside the door was a narrow slot which, on his side, fed into a wire bin. It was close to overflowing with parcels and letters.

Schmidt knew physical mail was an anachronism and that others might go months without receiving a single item of post. Another privilege, then, like the coffee. Perhaps they were keeping this service functioning solely for him? Perhaps there was someone out there whose job consisted exclusively of sorting and delivery his mail?

If so, Schmidt wondered if they were grateful for their employment, or if they were among the multitude of his detractors.

* * *

It wasn't as if he hadn't considered the problem before that conversation with Kahn. Or so Schmidt assured himself. He was unwilling to admit his sudden obsession had anything to do with their relationship, or some residue of feeling from their brief, historically distant attempt at a sexual partnering. All he knew was that she'd challenged him at a moment when he was seeking challenge.

That night, Schmidt lay awake, listening to the thrum of the turbines on the hill and continuing the inconclusive argument in his head.

There's nature, he said, *and nurture. What we begin as and what we experience. That's all there is and all there can be.*

Not so, Kahn responded. *For automatons, maybe. Maybe for ants. But to make a human being, a creature of infinite complexity and endless capacity, you need something more. You should know that better than anyone, Paul. Show me the software engineer who's made a program that can really think.*

But Schmidt had already, through his construct of Kahn, led himself into an avenue he didn't wish to pursue. It was true artificial intelligence had yet to make the leap to what could be universally perceived as intellect. It was true, in fact, that they seemed to have struck an invisible wall, one that resisted even the second-gen organic computers being perfected in the increasingly ironically named Silicon Valley. If the definition of intelligence was human sentience, then Kahn was correct; there was a missing part, a key refusing to be found.

Mentally, Schmidt pursued a different tack. *What does AI have to do with it? There might be a hundred reasons we can't create something we recognise as intelligence. How often over the centuries have we failed to acknowledge it in our own kind? No, the question isn't whether, through egotism, we should deny the stamp of intelligence to anything but ourselves; it's whether what we regard as intelligence can be quantified to the ultimate degree.*

In its components, Kahn said, *of course it can. To an extent, psychiatry is purely the business of identifying and predicting the patterns that conduct human nature. But that proves nothing. There'll always be a final surprise, an x-factor. Take a personality you know intimately, give them a hundred choices, and ninety-nine times you might see their answer coming, but on the hundredth they'll defy you.*

Then the tools are inadequate, Schmidt countered. *Psychology is inadequate, psychiatry doubly so. With the right tool, there'd be no anomalous hundredth answer... no thousandth, no ten-thousandth. With the right tool used in the right manner, there'd be no dark corner left for this soul of yours to hide in.*

He was starting to drift, wakefulness confusing with the peripheries of sleep, and in his mind, Schmidt saw her: black hair cut short, age-lines noticeable around eyes the shade of polished walnut as she edged closer to 50, though hardly diminishing her stubborn attractiveness. The scene was as it had been earlier that day, but now it was night outside the coffee shop, and all he saw clearly was her face leaning toward his.

Prove it, she told him, his imaginary re-enactment of her, his straw woman. *Prove it. Prove it if you can.*

* * *

Schmidt carried the pile of mail indoors and into his study, where he separated letters from parcels, which would need to be checked with the scanner the police had given him. But the last attempted bombing had been long ago, and since then, the contents had grown less obviously threatening, though stranger: mementos of broken lives, copies of books—often religious—and sometimes, rarely, gifts from sympathetic well-wishers.

It was always interesting to be reminded that not everyone despised him, that there were a few who considered him a saviour. Yet their communications were no more comforting than the other sort. The haters had turned away from his creation, but those others, the minority who sent him missives of thanks, of praise, of painful relief, had embraced it, and in so doing had become terrifying.

Schmidt sat at his desk, opening his mail as they'd trained him to, testing for anything that might be a wire, glass, a sachet of powder. But he found only letters, and those were quite bad enough.

* * *

When he woke the next morning, the conversations with Kahn, both real and imaginary, were blurring, but the problem was sharp and clear. And already he had ideas, as though they'd gestated in his sleeping thoughts.

There was chance. That was one facet. It was accepted that there was no such thing, that the universe was a great, intricate machine made of great and intricate machines. The body was a machine, the mind too. Their movements, tickings, pulsations, were predictable. Sometimes it might appear otherwise, especially when one prodded into the deepest, most chaotic-seeming strata of reality, but research brought understanding, and understanding made the eccentric reliable.

As he ate a breakfast of grapefruit, rye bread, and green tea, Schmidt brought up a SynApps screen and studied the rhythms of his own body. He watched multi-coloured lines soar and veer, abstracting the workings of his innards into rainbow mountain ranges. He was eating grapefruit, which he despised, because studies indicated it was a good preventer of heart disease, and recently his MeDiag software had announced that he was staring down a heart attack if he failed to reform his diet. With a degree of tweaking, the program could surely predict the month, if not the week or even the day, in which, if the warning went unheeded, his heart would abandon its struggle. And the software was continually advancing. How long before it could anticipate the precise moment in which the hypothetical became real?

The MeDiag software wasn't the only predictor of human circumstance, far from it. There were cameras everywhere, in public and private. All of them were capable of matching faces to identities and all reported to the NSA's data-forts and other huge information resources, which were then scoured and sorted by AIs, including the corporate mega-AIs that analysed and predicted market tendencies down to the household level. There were children in the world who'd spent 90 per cent of their lives beneath the gaze of that immense, information-hoarding hydra. And didn't the schools and most of the multinationals keep psych profiles? Wasn't gene-mapping for new-borns more and more common?

There was a wealth of information out there, an overabundance. And much of it was in the corporate-public domain, that vast grey area that the university's connections allowed him access to, if only he could make a persuasive case. Therefore, the problem wasn't finding the resources for what he had in mind but justifying his requirement—which meant concocting an application, a purpose to bring that treasure trove of data together.

* * *

Schmidt took the first letter from the pile. He didn't read all of them, but he made a point of at least sampling them, though he'd utterly exhausted their possibilities. There were definite trends, and a handful of individuals who wrote constantly, reiterating the same notions with stubborn persistence.

This was from one of the haters. It opened with a bizarrely polite *Dear Dr Schmidt*, and continued:

I picture you sometimes, sitting in your ivory tower, looking down on us, us ants. I wonder if you use it yourself. I've decided you must. Sometimes time seems to jumble and I wonder if it told you you'd do what you did, if it warned you you'd be the one, like a loop that goes on without any way out. If that was the case, then none of this would be your fault, and I couldn't blame you. But I do.

I would say I hope you die, but I suppose you know by now whether you will or won't, and my saying so won't make a milligram of difference. And it wouldn't change things anyway. Still, I do hope.

The letter finished with an equally courteous and inappropriate *Yours Sincerely,* then a name he'd come to recognise, Marjorie Southerland. An old-fashioned name. An old woman's name. Also, the letter was hand-written—and, of course, was a *letter*—all of which pointed to an older person.

But Schmidt tried to remember what the police detective had said, back when this started, back when such letters had shaken him to his core: 'You need not to think about it. There are crazy people out there. You can't imagine how crazy some people get.'

So maybe Marjorie Southerland was a middle-aged man writing out of his parents' basement. Whoever they were, though, they were wrong. Schmidt hadn't looked at it in years. He didn't need to be told the patterns of his life; he knew them all too well.

* * *

By the time his application for the necessary data permissions was complete, Schmidt had determined what his core technology would be. His friend Roebech had been working on it for almost three years, and Schmidt realised now that the memory of that fact had been informing his reasoning all along.

Roebech had started out in the AI gold rush, the tidal wave of funding that had swept the world when faith that synthetic intelligences would come to drive every technology was at its height. And Roebech, like many, had nearly gone under when the bubble inevitably burst.

However, Roebech had been fast enough on his feet to repurpose his ideas into something more provably useful. As he'd once observed to Schmidt, 'The problem was never creating a machine that can think; we did that in every meaningful sense ten years ago. The problem is making a machine some idiot bean-counter can *see* thinking.'

So instead, Roebech had selected one aspect of his work and focused on that: artificial learning, with an emphasis on pattern recognition and interpretation.

Schmidt approached him on the morning of the day he was due to put the application in. He simply hadn't dared before; without Roebech's technology, he had nothing.

'What would your construct do,' he said, 'if it was fed data—both historical and live data—on a single subject? On a person?'

Roebech, evidently surprised by the question, replied, 'In its current form? Not a lot. But with a little tweaking...'

'Yes?' Schmidt tried fiercely to hide his hope.

'Well, it would do what I've designed it to do. It would learn that person. It would learn until it understood them.'

And Schmidt released the breath he'd been holding. He let Roebech in on his plans then, or at least the parts Roebech would find engaging. The challenge would excite him, at any rate. He'd been growing obviously frustrated in recent months, striving to pinpoint applications for his learning construct outside the usual outlets. What he was developing had much in common, after all, with the pseudo-AIs with which the multinationals sifted their slag heaps of consumer information. But nothing like that appealed to Roebech.

Schmidt's project, however... *that* appealed, all right. It might even have been exactly what he was looking for.

The proposal went in. Schmidt was careful to emphasise the commercial utility, the potential for hyper-detailed focus groups and such, but he wasn't so naive as to ignore other applications. Wouldn't military contractors, for example, be glad of a technology that revealed how a soldier would react before they knew themselves?

Schmidt didn't ever discover who his mysterious benefactor was. He was never interested. Scientific morality was all well and good, but whatever department he made his creation for, it would find its way to others quickly enough. If he designed it for the private sector, it would eventually be repurposed by the state, and vice versa. To him, where the money came from was irrelevant.

* * *

The second letter he picked had no salutation and no name. It read, *f8 told me to write this so I'm writing it. f8 said this was what I'd write and I've written it how it said. I'm sorry for all the letters. I don't like writing them and I don't want to write again but probably I will.* The handwriting resembled a child's, which clenched Schmidt's heart for an instant.

He'd barely grazed the pile, but he pushed it aside nevertheless. Perhaps he'd return to it later. More plausibly, when he came back to his study in the evening, he'd gaze at the stacked letters with a sense of gnawing discontent, then tip them into the recycler.

There was other mail to deal with: the electronic kind familiar to the vast majority of Earth's inhabitants. Yet even there, Schmidt clung wilfully to the past. He preserved a physical screen and keyboard, when almost everyone had adopted virtualised equivalents. Schmidt considered the machine an intrusion, and was less likely to explore his electronic than his physical mail.

Today, he felt, would be one of the days he ignored it altogether. He couldn't say why, since it was no more hysterical or recriminatory than most, but that second letter had shaken him. He very much wanted to go back to bed.

Then he heard the noise. It was muffled by intermediary walls, piercing and mulishly electronic, and it took him a long moment to identify.

It was the ringing of a telephone.

* * *

They never learned how their technology got out. But there was no question it was Schmidt's work. His digital signature—and Roebech's, and those of others on the staff—were embedded in the core code. Chiefly Schmidt's, though; his name was everywhere. And he knew the thief could have removed it and hadn't. They'd made that choice.

It had been out for weeks before he heard. When he did, it was via agents of a government section he didn't recognise, some branch of the NSA or CIA. They were very polite. They appreciated that he hadn't leaked his own project, and no-one was blaming him for any laxity in the university's security. But *he* needed to appreciate that they had their jobs to do, and that it was best if he grasped from the outset how little say he had in the matter.

This they told Schmidt while he sat dumbstruck, panic bubbling in his stomach. He was afraid for the loss of months of work, and nervous of the men in their dark suits. But perhaps also he had a small intuition of what he'd done—of what he'd let loose.

Or perhaps not. The way they described it, it sounded harmless enough. His program, in its illegally modified form, had started life as scarcely more than a toy. It had been released as a SynApps plug-in, an application for the DNI wetware devices which had increasingly dominated computing in recent years. It was called simply f8.

The name wasn't his. He hadn't named his creation, besides the departmental tag he was obliged to use. f8 sounded like the street name of some recreational drug, and he supposed it had become precisely that. Just as once Ecstasy had begun as MDMA, 3,4-methylenedioxy-N-methylamphetamine, used to relieve pain and depression, so f8 had been project SOMA-931-A-77: a mouthful, to be sure, but a name without such awful, awesome connotations.

The drug comparison was fair. A recreational stimulant, that was f8 in its first incarnation. All it did was suggest statistical likelihoods: *there's an 87 per cent chance you'll have tuna in your lunchtime sandwich today*, that kind of thing.

Harmless. A game. But people were latching onto it. Its remarkable accuracy intrigued them, and there was fun to be had in choosing whether to accept f8's verdicts or rebel against them—to rebel, in effect, against the patterns of one's own behaviour.

Nobody had questioned how it did what it did, or where it drew its data from, or whether those resources were ones it had a legal right to, not until f8 had finally come to the government's attention. And by then, it was much too late.

* * *

The telephone was another anachronism. But Schmidt had spent a great deal of money and effort isolating his SynApps install, refining its external links to the barest necessities, and the police had insisted he have some means of being contacted and of contacting them in turn.

He hadn't used the phone in months, perhaps years. He couldn't remember where he'd left it. It droned and droned until he found it beneath a pile of papers in a corner of the permanently vacant guest bedroom. He was hesitant to pick up, and equally anxious that its strident complaints would cease and he'd never know who'd tried to contact him.

His fear was that they'd be someone akin to the letter writers and the protesters outside the gates, who only wished to spew their vitriol. Yet it was unlikely such people could have got the number. He'd given it to no-one except the police. And now he didn't recall how long the phone had been ringing, how long it was programmed to trill for before it gave up.

In panic, Schmidt snatched at the device. He placed the sliver of curved plastic to his ear, saying nothing, and heard a rhythmic sighing like the distant ocean.

Then: 'Hello?'

A woman's voice, familiar. 'Kahn?' he said, astonished.

'Paul? Is that you?' She sounded older than when he'd last spoken to her—as must he.

'It's me,' Schmidt admitted. 'How did you get this number?'

'From the police. It took some doing.'

'They shouldn't have given it out.' Realising he was being ungracious, Schmidt added, 'But if I'd thought, I'd have asked them to make an exception.'

She didn't answer immediately, and when she was silent, there was solely the muted oceanic roar. Just as he was starting to imagine there might be sense or a pattern there, she said, 'I was always sorry about how we left things. And I wanted to get in touch. But you made it so difficult.'

'Most of the people who want to contact me aren't my friends,' Schmidt pointed out.

'I know that. I can see how it must have been for you. It's dreadful and unfair. I know I blamed you, like those idiots do. I was wrong, and I'm sorry. Nobody should have to live the way you have.'

'It's all right,' he said.

'No. It isn't.' Clearly, she'd made her mind up. And when Kahn made up her mind, there was no changing it.

'Fine,' he said, 'it isn't. But, whatever you or those people outside my gates or anyone else might believe, I *did* bring this on myself. I had a responsibility and I abused it.'

He'd never put this into words. Maybe he'd never consciously admitted it, though on some level he'd known since that meeting with the government agents. 'In my opinion, isolation is a small price to pay.'

'It's inhumane,' Kahn said. 'Anyway, I'm taking the decision out of your hands. You're going to come and have coffee with me.'

Strangely, Schmidt's first thought was not of whether he wanted to go, nor even of Kahn, but of the protestors. Could he get past them? He remembered that there was the rear gate, but felt no relief. 'I'll have to think about it.'

'No, you won't. If you think, you'll talk yourself out of it. Say yes, and be ready at 12 o'clock tomorrow.'

There was no doubt in her tone. It would be so easy to agree. 'I'll think about it.'

'Paul...'

'I promise,' Schmidt said, 'I'll think about it and get back to you.'

* * *

It only took a few months for f8 to begin to change.

In the meantime, both the university and the government fought it, in their different ways and for their different reasons. They tried to wipe it out, found it unstoppable as every digital plague before, unstoppable as wildfire: stamp it down in one place and it burned twice as brightly in another. They cut off its accesses, only to unearth new links, new leaks. They tried to make it illegal, found themselves wallowing in red tape. And, for all that, they hadn't quite seen the danger—though perhaps they'd caught its scent on the wind.

Schmidt saw. A scattering of others too. Kahn was among them. Their arguments escalated—and eventually, erupted. She blamed him, and increasingly he felt she was correct to.

Because f8 was improving. Of course it was. With Roebech's AI engine at its heart, it was designed to learn until it knew its subject perfectly, and that was exactly what it was doing.

For such a long time, f8 was a game. Then it grew into a convenience. So many decisions were too minor to be worth making; better to ask f8 what you'd do rather than take the trouble to decide. And every user was connected. How useful it was to pre-empt when a job offer would be made, when a lover would finally walk out. After all, there remained the choice, if you chose to take it. However great a percentage, f8 still left other possibilities.

Then one day there were no more possibilities.

That day, millions of people consulted f8, to find the program they'd come to rely on for guidance no longer guiding. That day, they were offered not probabilities but certainties.

Inevitably, there were factors f8 couldn't predict: a subway train breaking down, freak weather events. But it was gathering information from a multitude of sources, not just its flesh-and-blood subjects with their histories, their medical records and diagnostics, their genetic data, and the constant surveillance of their lives, but a thousand databases on every subject that might impact human behaviour. It wasn't always right, but it was right the vast majority of times—and it was perpetually expanding.

Worst, though, was how f8 compensated for its own existence. For months, it had observed reactions to its predictions, like a teacher surveilling a class of unruly students. It anticipated rebellion. It knew when to expect resistance. It foresaw the reactions its predictions would provoke, predicted according to those reactions. It knew when you'd consult it. It told you. In a sense, it was the perfect drug: reliance created greater reliance, on and on without end.

Many swore off it—though uninstalling the program, let alone keeping it uninstalled, was another matter entirely. Some went the other way. The first cases of addiction were reported within a week. The first related suicide came soon after. Even among those who believed they couldn't live without f8, there were plenty who discovered they couldn't live with it either.

They never found the perpetrator, the thief who'd stolen Schmidt's creation and moulded it into something insidious and terrible. There were days when Schmidt wondered if f8 had leaked itself. Roebech had once, in a drunken panic, intimated the same. And drunk or sober, he wouldn't answer Schmidt's questions about what purpose his software had originally been designed for, what applications he'd cannibalised to create it.

At any rate, Schmidt had won his debate with Kahn. No-one much talked about the human soul anymore, or even of free will. Schmidt had created a light so bright that nothing could be kept from it.

He was in hiding by then, had been since the first clumsy murder attempt. It was already apparent that he'd surely be in hiding for whatever remained of his life.

* * *

He would like to see Kahn.

Of all his friends, he'd missed her most. But to go outside, to dare the protesters, to risk being recognised... Schmidt's stomach revolted at those prospects. He understood that he'd become agoraphobic, but the understanding didn't help. The fear reaction was too overwhelming.

However, for the first time in a long while, he was conscious of his aloneness. He'd made himself grow used to it, but acceptance had been easy when there was no alternative. Now that he had a choice, he could feel the isolation of spirit that had kept him sane slipping away. Kahn had taken it with a few brief words, and he resented her for that deeply, was simultaneously grateful.

He would like to go outside. He'd like to see Kahn. He was afraid to leave the house, horrified at the notion of making conversation. It was a hard decision. And it was ages since he'd made any decision at all.

Schmidt made a fresh pot of coffee. He took a cup into his study and waved the antiquated computer on, half thinking he might start on his emails. His finger hovered over the icon, but the idea of wading through more hatred appalled him. He should go ahead and delete the lot, he thought—and was surprised at himself.

Perhaps he was only trying to divert his deliberation away from Kahn. Such a hard decision. Even considering it was like exerting an atrophied muscle.

Then he realised why he'd sat at the computer, and which icon his finger had gravitated toward.

He'd done his best to remove it all those years ago. It had fought him to a stalemate. Would it still work? It was out of date, cut off from its wider connections, but it was probably synchronising with his SynApps install. It still knew him, better than he ever could know himself.

So hard to decide. Such a torment. And so unnecessary. Yet here was another decision, the decision not to decide. Was it any easier?

Beneath his finger, the icon was brutally simple in its design: just those two characters, f and 8, intertwined.

As though paralysed, Schmidt's finger hung.

The Epsilon Requirement

Caroline Misner

I can honestly say that, of all the maniacs and despots I've been forced to babysit, Napoleon was one of the most pompous little pricks I'd ever encountered. He had the same stunned expression as all the others when he dropped—head jerking side to side, eyes wide and unblinking as he took in the walls of the alcove.

When he saw me, he lunged, pulling a sabre from a sheath at his belt. By then I had grown accustomed to having my charges attack me, but I must admit, this time I flinched. A few of the others had their weapons with them when they dropped, and I was easily able to defend myself.

Napoleon stopped short just inches away from me, raised the sabre and screamed, 'Qui est-tu? Ou suis-je?'

I regretted not paying more attention in high school French. Back then, I thought my chances of ever stepping foot in France were next to zero, so I slacked off and barely passed.

I juggled a sentence around in my mind, trying to remember my first day in class. I must have sounded stilted and heavily accented to anyone fluent in French, but I had to keep him calm.

'Je m'appelle,' I said, tapping my chest, '...John. John Wildish.'

'John Wildish?' Napoleon lowered his sabre and eyed me warily. 'Et-tu Anglais?'

I nodded and answered, 'Oui... English.'

Napoleon sheathed his sabre, raised his chin and thumped his chest.

'Je m'appelle Napoleon!' he declared proudly.

I don't know if he expected me to be impressed with that. I could have shaken his hand, bowed like a toady or grovelled at his feet, but none of that would have mattered anymore. Even if I was fluent in French, I couldn't have explained our situation to him in a way he would understand. I could barely comprehend it myself.

'Anglais? Bah!' Napoleon barked when I didn't respond with anything more than a cursory nod. 'Suis-je capture?'

I didn't understand but I didn't need to. I sat cross-legged on the floor and patted the spot beside me, inviting him to sit. Napoleon smirked and turned away, pacing back and forth with his hands clasped behind his back and his shoulders hunched. He looked nothing like the portraits I'd seen of him. Whoever the artists were, they had been very kind. Though he wasn't as short as I expected, his hairline was receding. His features were softer, almost girlish, and the downward hook at the tip of his nose was more prominent, almost touching his upper lip.

'Garcon! J'ai soif!' he said, 'Obtenez-moi de l'eau.'

I had no idea what he said so I shook my head and shrugged.

'Stupide!' Napoleon tapped his knuckles on the side of his head.

That I understood. I'd learned through painful experience how dangerous it could be to confront the captives, but this time something inside my head finally sprung. I jumped to my feet and stared right into those intense, beady little eyes.

'Listen,' I said. 'You may have been the hot shit back in seventeenth century France or whenever, but here you're nothing, a nobody. I can't do anything for you other than keep you company. I'm a prisoner as much as you are. Soon you'll be meeting Golfish and, trust me, he's not as nice as I am. So I suggest you sit down and shut up before I really lose my cool with you!'

Napoleon startled back, hands up in defence. I don't think he was used to having anyone challenge him like that. I almost felt like the Duke of Waterloo.

When Napoleon regained his composure, he made drinking motions with his cupped hand. 'L'eau. L'eau.'

'Water.' I nodded. 'You want water. That's no problem. Follow me.'

It wasn't unusual for new arrivals to drop thirsty. Whatever process Golfish used to snag them through the threads of time must have been dehydrating. Napoleon stood his ground when I headed toward one of the entrances to the tunnels and I had to beckon him to follow. I can't say I blame him. Those passages were cloaked with some sort of black fog that I had to pass through each time I wanted a drink or food or to take a leak.

Each tunnel led to the same spot: another detention chamber with a rough cylindrical monolith in the centre that reached up toward some black-shrouded altitude. Cold water flowed down it and pooled at its base where it drained into depths unknown. It was the only water I had for drinking and washing. Although I tried to keep myself clean with what little I had, I would have traded my soul for a nice hot shower.

Narrow shelves lined the walls and, if I was lucky, I would find a scrap of soap or a dull razor. Once I found a toothbrush and I'm sure wherever Golfish was, he watched me as I brushed my teeth, fascinated with what humans did with toothbrushes. I was tempted to give him a real show, but I changed my mind, knowing I would have to put it back in my mouth again.

I ran my fingers through the waterfall and said, 'Here's all the water we need. We have no cups, so you'll have to use your hands. If you need to take a leak, go in the puddle at the bottom.'

Napoleon gazed around the chamber, looking both astounded and terrified. 'Ou sommes nous?' he asked.

I tugged his sleeve and guided his hand into the waterfall. He slurped loudly as he scooped the water into his mouth.

When he finished drinking, he splashed water over his face and combed it through his hair with his fingers.

'Feel better?' I asked. 'Want something to eat?'

I must give credit to Golfish for never allowing me to go hungry, though the food was deplorable—hard little biscuits that tasted like a combination of shredded cardboard and birdseed. I'd complained to Golfish once and he assured me that those biscuits were the perfect balance of all nutrients needed to keep a human alive. And why not? After all, if I'm your little captive canary I may as well be fed on pellets. I pulled a biscuit from one of the shelves and showed it to Napoleon.

'It's all we've got,' I said.

I broke a chunk off with my teeth, trying not to grimace as I chewed. Napoleon sniffed the piece I gave him and licked it with the tip of his tongue before taking a bite. He immediately spat it out.

'I know it tastes like shit,' I said, 'but it's guaranteed to keep you alive.'

Napoleon looked at me as though I was crazy to eat such a thing, so I thought of one of the few words I remembered from Introduction to French 101.

'Merde,' I said. 'This tastes like *merde.*'

'Merde?' Napoleon asked.

'Oui,' I replied. 'It tastes like shit.'

Then Napoleon did the one thing I never would have imagined. He laughed. It was so infectious I laughed myself for the first time since my arrival. Perhaps this pretentious little son of a bitch wouldn't be such bad company after all.

We sat on the floor in the alcove and gnawed our rations. The wall was rough, and I padded my back with my haversack so I could lean against it. Napoleon scanned his surroundings. There wasn't much to see—rocky blank walls and a ceiling so high you couldn't see it.

Sallow light seeped from fissures in the walls. Once I peered into one of the cracks and a sharp pain stabbed my eye and nearly blinded me. It was a thousand times worse than getting your picture taken with one of those old-fashioned flash cameras and I never did it again.

Golfish was very good at keeping his cages secure.

I tried to explain to Napoleon how we both ended up as specimens in Golfish's menagerie. I had been unceremoniously dumped on Golfish's proverbial doorstep by an unscrupulous Wrill and sold like chattel. Golfish needed another human. His last one had been eaten by some beast from a planet I'd never heard of when Golfish mistakenly believed humans could endure the caustic liquid the beast poured over its prey before slurping them up like soup.

Communicating with Golfish was unlike anything I had ever experienced. Having no mouth or nose or any other discernible features, he conversed telepathically, blasting symbols into my mind. His physical body was repulsive, reminding me of the Silly Putty I played with as a kid—blobby and stretchy with a stubby tail that tapered at the bottom. He floated about in mid-air though there was no evidence of wings or propellers or any other sort of flying apparatus on him. When I questioned him, I blinked on an image of a kids' birthday party balloon, wrinkled with age and bobbing through the air. So Golfish was full of gas.

An image of my old friend, Bucky the one-horned goat, flashed into my mind. Bucky stood in a stall with a very pregnant and very agitated mare. His presence calmed her and she lowered her head until her muzzle touched his single corrugated horn. I wanted to know why Golfish would need me for such a situation.

A field of opened books flashed into my consciousness. Thousands and thousands of books spreading as far as I could see. The pages flipped and fanned, showing images of people from various points in history—admirals, Caesars, generals, all dressed in full military regalia of their time. There were images of shabbily dressed street thugs and mafia dons and other lesser-known hoodlums that seemed so important to Golfish.

I shook my head to rattle some comprehension into it. What would he need with them—and more importantly, how would he obtain them without radically altering the history of the human race? An appendage that was definitely not human reached into the flapping pages of one of the books and plucked out a page with Genghis Khan's image on it before allowing the rest of the pages to continue falling, all with pictures of Genghis Khan going about his daily life. A light wind lifted the page from the appendage, and it landed in my hand. I closed my fingers on it and felt the page crinkle into a ball. Whatever I had seen was an obvious mirage. But this was real.

The wrinkled old balloon bobbed back into my field of vision, surrounded by miniatures of those historical figures. They were not alone. Thousands of other creatures joined them—Wrills, Morbians, Nomads—the spindly-limbed bulbous-headed humanoids that first come to mind when you think about aliens. Specimens of just about every sentient creature that inhabits the galaxy and beyond.

There must have been no image that Golfish could have planted into my mind to explain his motives. He expressed it with words I still don't understand: *they have the Epsilon Requirement*.

Flashes of battles throughout history zipped through my mind, images of horrible violence—hacked limbs, severed heads, screams of the defeated as they lay dying, queues of innocents marching to their doom. And blood. Everywhere there was blood, split bellies spilling organs, people with half their lower bodies blown off crawling futilely toward safety.

I screamed, truly afraid for the first time since my arrival and begged Golfish to make the images stop. I would go mad if I had to witness any more.

So he was amassing his own personal army of the best warlords throughout the history of the universe. I was needed to keep the humans calm until he snatched them from our holding cell and sent them for orientation and training. What he had planned to do with all of us was beyond me.

The violent images mercifully stopped and the ground below me melted away until I toppled into nothingness. I spiralled through the air of whatever planet I was on. Huge, tunnelled mounds spread out as far as I could see like a field of ant hills. I plunged headlong into the opening of one of the tunnels like Alice in Wonderland twirling down the rabbit hole and landed hard in the cell where I have been ever since.

Napoleon stared at me so hard and so long, I thought for a second he had lapsed into a coma. I don't know if he had understood me or not. When he finally moved, he heaved his shoulders, sighed and hung his head.

'Je suis damnee,' he said.

So Golfish had brought down the mighty Napoleon. At least it was a comfort knowing that through all the layers of space and time, there are infinite Napoleons, in infinite universes, each creating their own histories. And there are infinite mes, living all the lives I could have lived if I hadn't existed on this particular thread. I was back in my dorm room, laptop on knees, cramming for an exam. Or I was married to Becky Bishop, my first love, and starting a family. Or I was backpacking through the mountains of Tibet. I am anywhere and everywhere.

I tried to rouse Napoleon, but he shuffled away from me and buried his face in his hands. This pompous little douche-bag was more cowardly than I expected. Just as Ivan the Terrible had been when he dropped. After I managed to pry his filthy fingers off my neck, he collapsed in a heap of sobs and remained a quivering ball until he lifted out.

The bravest captive had been a warrior named Boudicca. I think she must have been some sort of Viking Queen, but whoever she was, she was one bad-assed bitch. Wonder Woman would look like a girl scout beside her. She dropped wearing a full set of armour, complete with sword and shield. I didn't even realise she was a woman until she removed her helmet to get a better look at me.

Her wild red hair was filthy and twisted in long dishevelled braids. She pointed the tip of her sword at my throat and babbled in some ancient language. She was the first woman to have dropped and I was afraid Golfish was experimenting with some bizarre mating ritual. This bitch could have ripped me in half. I indicated with gestures that I didn't understand and showed her I was unarmed and just as much a prisoner.

Once she calmed and accepted her fate, she became almost a substitute mother, making sure I was eating enough and that I was clean and comfortable. I slept with my head in her lap with Boudicca on lookout for anything that might attack us. When the howls and grunts of the other captives echoed down through the tunnels, she would pass me her shield and raise her sword, standing between me and the tunnels, ready to take on whatever dared to approach us.

When it was time for her to lift out, she dropped to one knee and bowed her head as she handed me her sword. I couldn't take it. I gestured that wherever she was going, she would need it more than me. She seemed to understand because she nodded and rose to her feet. And then she lifted out and was gone.

'We must escape.' Napoleon's accent was thick but comprehensible. I startled back, more enraged than surprised.

'You speak English?' I demanded. The last captive who spoke English, albeit in a heavy Brooklyn drawl, had been Al Capone, and that had been a long time ago.

'Oui.' Napoleon nodded.

'Why didn't you tell me?' I said. 'I've been babbling like an idiot all this time.'

'I never interrupt an enemy when he is in the middle of making a mistake,' Napoleon replied.

'I'm not your enemy!' I shouted. 'But I could be.'

I had never attacked any of the others before, but Napoleon pushed me to the brink. I lunged at him, hoping to grab his stubby neck and strangle him the way Ivan the Terrible had tried to do to me.

'Wait!' Napoleon dodged my grasp and backed up against the nearest wall. 'Please. We can work together.'

'I can't trust you, you little shit!' I swung at him, and he ducked.

'You must!' Napoleon said.

'Even if I could, there's no way out of here,' I said.

'There is always a way,' Napoleon said and pointed at the limitless ceiling. 'If there is a way in, there is way out. We come from there, no?'

'We would never make it,' I replied. 'I've tried.'

'Then perhaps from there?' Napoleon pointed to one of the tunnel entrances where the crackly language of some alien species echoed like popping bubbles. 'There are others, no?'

'We can't reach them and they can't reach us,' I said. 'Besides, we don't know who they are or where they come from. They could be dangerous.'

'Nonsense!' Napoleon drew his sabre. 'I have a weapon!'

Napoleon ran wildly down one of the tunnels, the black fog swallowing him like a lozenge. He wasn't the first to try dashing down the tunnels in a futile effort at escape and he probably wouldn't be the last. Most of the captives had done that at one time or another, even Boudicca. I don't know how

Golfish had managed it, but every tunnel led back to the chamber. Napoleon emerged from the opposite tunnel, sabre raised and looking baffled to find himself back where he started. Someone or something grunted behind him.

'I told you,' I said. 'There is no way out.'

'But there must be!' Napoleon declared and charged down another tunnel. When he emerged on the opposite side, he tried another tunnel—and then another and another. He tried all of them in turn, only to find himself, winded and bewildered, back in the chamber with me. I must give him kudos for his tenacity. All the others had given up after only a few tries.

It was a long time before a breathless Napoleon finally gave up and dropped to his knees, hands bunched in frustration.

'Golfish decides when we leave,' I said and heaved him back to his feet.

'Napoleon answers to no-one!' he declared. He must have lifted out before his defeat at Waterloo and his exile. I almost pitied the little prick. He'd had no idea what lay in store for him.

'All we can do is wait,' I said.

I rummaged through my haversack. It was the one thing from home I had managed to keep with me, stuffed with the last of my precious belongings from my former life: pens, scraps of paper, my wallet, keys to a car I would never drive again. There were keys to a dorm room where I used to sleep, a room I prayed I would awaken in and discover all this had been nothing more than a bad dream. I had my iPod and cell phone, both long since drained of power and utterly useless. I had shown them to many of the captives to amuse them and pass the time. Boudicca had been especially fascinated with a tube of lip balm that she smeared over her face with sighs of satisfaction.

'I bet you've never seen anything like this before.' I handed Napoleon an old, wrinkled wrapper from a granola bar. He sniffed it and tossed it back to me with a look of disgust.

'Do you have anything we can use to escape?' he asked.

'Believe me, I've tried,' I said. 'Here, look at this. It's called a comb. You could probably use it.'

'La peigne! I know what that is, you imbécile!'

I usually feel the vibration first. It starts as a tingling down near the bottom of my spine and slowly works its way up my back and leaches into my bones. By the time the other captives begin to feel it too, my nerves are tingling and nervous butterflies are scattering in my stomach. It's not that unpleasant a sensation, similar to the feeling you get while plunging down a roller coaster. Since I never lift out, I could only imagine how intense it must feel for the captives.

'I feel ill!' Napoleon clutched his middle and looked like he was going to puke.

'It's time.' My voice quivered from the vibration. I tightened the latch on my haversack. 'Just relax. Golfish is taking you now.'

Napoleon swallowed down whatever bile bubbled up his throat and tried to regain some composure. He looked up at the ceiling and raised his sabre the full length of his arm. That familiar greenish beam streamed down on him like a spotlight.

Napoleon knocked the wind out of me. I never would have guessed such an average-sized man could be so strong. He grabbed me by the waist and clutched me against him so hard, the embroidery on his jacket scratched my cheek. I couldn't struggle away. That green beam had some sort of paralysing effect.

'Vive, Napoleon!' he shouted at whoever or whatever was above us.

And we lifted out. Together.

Cracks of light whizzed by, the fissures widening until we were engulfed in blinding light. I could feel us rising, spiralling upward, higher and higher. As a kid I had nightmares of being trapped in runaway elevators that either plunged and shattered at the bottom of the shaft, or rose uncontrollably, up and up, faster and faster, until they burst through the ceiling. I screamed. Napoleon screamed, though it sounded more like a howl.

We landed hard on rocky ground that suddenly solidified beneath us. Napoleon dropped his sabre and landed on his ass, both legs tossing up before him. I fell on my knees, disoriented but grateful for the feel of solid ground.

We were on the surface of the planet. Mountains pocked with caves and tunnels loomed around us. Some were volcanic with vapour wisping from their summits. The sky was cloudless and dim, the colour of wet cardboard. The oxygen was so thin I could barely draw in a breath. Napoleon gasped and clutched his throat, cursing in French.

Golfish hovered over us, his long tapering tail twitching with confusion. He seemed genuinely surprised to see me there, though without any discernible features, it was difficult to judge his emotions. He floated in circles around us.

I had a vision of a pea sucked up a straw and popping from the top; another pea remained lodged in the bottom of the straw. I would have shouted at him that it was not my fault—Napoleon had grabbed me before I could break away, but my voice was little more than a squeak in the thin air.

Large bubbles bobbed around us. Each contained a pair of former captives that had lifted out. I recognised them all. Ivan the Terrible jousted with Jeffrey Dahmer. Vlad the Impaler locked swords with Mussolini. Pol Pot sparred with Joseph Stalin. Caligula was giving Hitler a good hard beating with his fists. Even my sweet protectress, Boudicca, waved her sword threateningly around Elizabeth Bathory's head. Bizarre combinations of some of the worst people in history paired up to fight one another in some sort of ludicrous gladiatorial games.

I felt dizzy from the lack of oxygen. I sucked in a breath deep enough to have burst my lungs back home and signalled Golfish to give me some air before I blacked out. A huge empty bubble descended over Napoleon. He instinctively leapt toward it and the bubble engulfed him like a fishbowl. He gulped in lungfuls of fresh air and colour returned to his ruddy face.

How I envied his ability to breathe!

Please! I begged Golfish in my mind, *Give me air! I need to breathe or I'll die.*

I don't know if Golfish had ever intended to keep me in one of his bubbles, but another empty one bounced around me and I lunged toward it. The bubble swallowed me into its depths, a warm moistness like passing through a temperate waterfall.

But there was air inside and I sucked in all I could.

Napoleon and I floated in our bubbles with Golfish swishing around us. He knew I would be no match for any of the other combatants. I'm not a professional warrior, and I like to think I'm not evil. I could never intentionally hurt anyone, no matter what despicable crimes they may have committed against humanity.

Napoleon pressed his hands against the walls of his bubble as though trying to break out.

I couldn't hear his words, but I knew what he said by the movements of his mouth. 'We must escape.'

I nodded but I was at a loss as to how. On the surface or burrowed underground, we were still Golfish's prisoners. I heaved my shoulder against the bubble in frustration and was surprised when it moved in that direction. I pushed again and again, and the bubble moved faster in whichever direction I leaned.

When Napoleon saw what I was doing, he began leaping around the inside of his bubble, jostling it and sending it zigzagging in different directions.

I pounced back and forth like a kid in a bouncy castle at a birthday party. My bubble rolled and bobbed and rose higher. Napoleon jumped and pushed his hands against the top of his bubble until it soared above me. I did the same until we hovered side by side, so high the others looked like miniatures in snow globes below us.

Golfish whizzed around us in a rage, trying to stop us or catch us with his whip-like tail. He loomed up the side of my bubble and peered at me. If he had a mouth, I'm sure he would have snarled. I snarled back and flipped him the bird.

'You lost an Epsilon, you motherfucker,' I said and knocked my bubble as hard as I could against Napoleon's.

Golfish's reaction was too slow. He missed Napoleon by mere inches as his balloon shot up, straight up into that flat featureless sky, higher and higher until his bubble was little more than a speck. Then he was gone.

I waved to him as he disappeared.

Golfish's tail elongated until his whole body thinned into an eely tentacle. He wrapped himself around my bubble and squeezed. I felt myself descend and my gut lurched up in my throat. Wherever Golfish was taking me, I knew I would survive.

After all, I was a hero.

I went down in history as the man responsible for releasing Napoleon into the universe

Buffalo Soldiers

Andrew Darlington

The frogs are singing. A huge moon hangs in the lazy slur of the night. The only colour is the splash of fire up ahead, framed by the trees. It forms the beacon I head for. As I push through shaggy reed tops higher than my head, I hear his song. Deep and resonant, richly spiritual, a voice weary with ancient suffering and endurance wrenched from the depths of his soul. A song so pure it rakes the stars, yearning for release, for deliverance from suffering.

The singer is one of four men who squat around the campfire. Buffalo soldiers, First Regiment Kansas Volunteer Infantry. Like me. I stand transfixed by the sheer beauty of his voice. As if to move will be to shatter the moment. It's only when the song ebbs to its final notes, and the silence closes in around us, that I stir.

They startle as I emerge, grabbing their carelessly laid-aside Burnside Carbines in scared haste, fumbling them around. Taking a bead. Until they get to see me more clearly.

'You lost, boy?' He wears a corporal's stripes beneath the epaulettes on his blue sleeve.

'I got separated. We saw action down Poison Spring way. Don't know what happened to the others.'

He slopes his rifle and slouches back down by the fire. 'We got coffee, brother. You want coffee?'

I grin my nervous gratitude, pause in hesitation, then move decisively across to join them. As though there's an option. There's a rusty triangular frame over the raw flames, with a can suspended. The water boils and steams. The spiderwork is condensation-slicked. The coffee smells so rich it sets my tastebuds a-dancing.

'It ain't healthy to go wandering around out there, no matter what rag you got on your back. Blue or grey makes no difference. There are white guys who string you up from the nearest magnolia like strange fruit for the sheer hell of it, as soon as they look at you.'

He says it with a wide grin as I set down beside them.

'That's Saul—he ain't much for talking, but he sure can sing up a storm, and that's Family Man,' he introduces us. 'And that's Runt. He ain't nothing but a kid, we watch out for him. Me, you can call me Corp.'

'Michael,' I respond, the glow of the flames hot on my cheek. I pause, wondering if I dare say more. 'You know something? We carry slave names. When our folks, and their folks were first stolen and brought in chains to this land of exile, when we was taken from our ancestral homeland, we had proud African names. They even took that from us. They stripped away our very identity.'

I gulp scalding coffee, taste the bitter gritty residue at the back of my teeth, and wait to see what reaction my words will provoke. 'When this war is over, in days as yet unborn, we shall reclaim everything that was once ours by right, everything that was stolen away from us.'

'A good question. For another time,' says the Corp.

'You're a thinking man. I can tell,' says Family Man with a leer. He smokes a long clay pipe he uses to stab the air, emphasizing his words. He spits a jet of discoloured phlegm between his teeth into the fire. 'You got a thinking head on those shoulders. I like that. But maybe if you wan keep that thinking head on them shoulders of yours, you best opt to pull in and duck down for some considerable time.'

Runt sits watching, all bones and awkwardness, his knees drawn up in an odd squatting position. Saul cleans his gun in a careful, meticulous way.

'You think this war is all about freedom, Michael? This war ain't nothin' about no freedom. This war is about one group of white folks feuding with another group of white folks. Nothing more or less than that, despite what the likes of ole abolitionist Frederick Douglass say. We just happen to be caught up in the middle. We dodge and dive as the wind blows. We make the best out of whatever we can. But don't you never believe for one heartbeat that everything's gonna change tomorrow or the day after tomorrow and usher in that shining Promised Land of the new day dawning.'

They laugh so hard the heat that burns my cheek comes not just from the fire. I'm eating, chewing what they're eating. I'm not even sure of what it is I'm eating. It might be squirrel. Something they hunted during their traipse down through the southland.

'I'm grateful. I'm truly grateful for your hospitality.'

'No sweat. You're an extra gun,' he shrugs. 'You can always report back to your unit whenever the hell we link up with someone who knows what's going on.'

'Thanks. I appreciate it.'

Runt is already sleeping. Something is howling out there in the darkness of the night. The frogs are singing. Corp stirs the fire in a way that makes it crack and spit a dancing column of bright sparks. As he feeds it fresh dry sticks, I catch the sharp aroma of charred wood.

'Family Man. You take first watch. Time for shut-eye.'

That night as we sleep, the ground beneath me is chilly and hard.

With morning, stiff with cramp, we kill the fire, kick dirt over the white ash of its smouldering embers, shoulder our packs and guns. Runt retreats into the trees and squats to shit, emerging with a big goofy grin, hoisting his braces back up over his uniform blouse.

Saul says nothing, just beams a slow smile. We straggle on in what the Corp insists is south, with the rising sun sending our shadows scuttling ahead to the edge of the trees. We keep the broad slow drawl of the river-drift to the right, sunflash on water, maybe it's lost its way too? Squelching through foul-smelling shallow marsh haunted by giant dragonflies, beneath the spread of fuzzy trees hung with Spanish moss.

Are there 'gators here? There are stinging bugs, small black flies that bite my neck and hands, until I get too weary to even bat them away. By noon we slope up onto a rutted trail, moving in a cautious arc. No need— there's no-one there.

Runt dances with an imaginary partner down the centre of the trail, circling and bowing to her as though it's a glittering ball at the Big House. Family Man laughs and throws rocks at him. Runt cusses and skips his agile dance out of the way.

Half a mile further there's a wagon approaching from the opposite direction, followed by a mule-drawn buckboard. It's a refugee family of poor-white sharecroppers. We watch them come. Move aside so they can pass. The old guy who sits high at the jangling reins nods in stern recognition. He has mutton-chop side-whiskers and wears a faded stovepipe hat. He has dirty bare feet. A woman in a bonnet peeps cautiously from behind the canvas flaps. She looks scared.

The Corp doffs his peaked cap. 'It's bad down the road apiece, Suh?'

'Soldiers,' grunts the old guy.

'Yank or Rebel?'

The old guy shrugs. 'Soldiers. Just soldiers.'

Then they're gone, and we continue.

'I smelled me dried fish,' says Family Man, sniffing the air grotesquely. 'They had a barrel of dried fish. Moonshine too, mayhaps?'

'Folks got to eat,' says the Corp.

He takes off his cap, and uses it to wipe wet from his forehead. I could smell no fish. Hunger plays games with the senses. But I could smell the horse and the sweat. I could smell the fear that hangs in the humid air. This is a time of terror.

But terrors that provide the taunting promise of freedom. Even when we try to deny it. We fight for it.

Almost before we realise it, there's a low bridge of old logs over a rushy creek that feeds into the broader swathe of the green river to the right. Stuck in the mud by the up-rise there's a grey gatling-gun, with four men heaving at it. They wear grey.

They turn.

They see us at the same moment we see them. They split in a panic. One levels a rifle. Family Man is quicker, takes him with a single shot. He pitches over the low log parapet into the brackish pool below. Saul takes a second Johnny Rebel in the back as he runs.

The other two stop. Raise their hands in slow resignation, and turn. The Corp grunts and spits. Shoots the first one in the forehead. A crimson blossom spouts above his startled eyes. He breech-loads a cartridge. Hits the second in the throat. The grey goes down coughing gouts of his life into the mud. The whole thing has taken little more than seconds.

The Corp turns to me, as though challenging me to accuse him. I'm too numb to say a word, caught in the stench of blood and cordite. A stink that slips down as hard as raw moonshine alcohol.

'How we gonna take captives?' he demands. 'Like we're in a position to take them prisoner, and escort them nicely back to the pen. Right?' His tone brooks no denial.

'Right Corp,' I concede uneasily.

'We're deep in the heart of Dixieland here. We strip them and turn them loose, they'll alert the county, that we're not only Union but black too. They gonna rip us apart piece by piece and use our bone-splinters to pick their teeth.'

He walks up to the rapid-fire gun and kicks mud from its big, trapped wagon-wheel mounting. Spins the un-ratcheted hand-crank around once, and again. 'We can't take it with us. No ammunition. No use to us. But we should wreck it so's it caint be used against us neither. Pity, it's a pretty machine. Wonder where they was hauling it from?'

'Or where they're hauling it to?' I look down the trail towards no-place in particular.

Family Man stoops low over the dead rebs. 'They're li'l more than kids. Looks to be about no more than fifteen. The Confederacy must be gettin' desperate if'n they're conscripting children.'

Runt is hawking into the river. He sounds like he's raw-spewing his guts. I feel the same sickness canting and squirming at my own bowels.

'I prefer to keep ma stomach empty until the business of the day is done,' says the Corp soberly.

We shin further down the creek-side to where it swirls out into the main body of the river. Turtles duck beneath weed and scud away out of sight. The Corp strips off his shirt and crouches, scooping up huge handfuls of clear water and lifting it dripping to sluice over his face and stream down his chest. There's a raised crisscross pattern of discoloured scar tissue covering every inch of his back.

'You're familiar with the taste of the lash.'

He turns big mournful eyes of the most flawless blue onto me. His face a dark leather caricature in shadow. 'We all got tales to tell, Michael. Ain't that the truth? I got mine. You certainly got yours. Tell me your truth. Testify. What you really doing here?'

'You're correct, Corp, for me, this is more than just that. This is a spiritual journey.'

He's crouched, so I'm standing above him. His eyes laying me open.

'I know this county,' I say. 'I've been here. This is not just water for me—it's blood, tears and sweat. We have history.'

He stands, wiping his hands, pulling his shirt back over his head.

'Knew it. Knew it all along. This is a personal thing. Let me guess. This is where you escape from, this is where you run and hide from all the way north. You got kin? You got scores to settle?'

I nod once, abruptly. As though reluctant to concede. 'Down the road apiece. No kin. Not any more. But more grudges than you'd believe. Wounds that time won't let heal.'

Family Man is there. I'd not noticed him approach. 'Who do you expect to find on the other side, Michael? A spiritual connectivity, like you've reached some better place.'

I feel trapped. First by my admission. Now by my inability to frame suitable words in reply.

I'd never heard Saul utter a word before. But when he does, his voice is as compelling as his song. 'When I talk to god, I think he understands. He says sit by my side, I'll be your god on hand.'

I'm not sure what he means. But I feel oddly soothed.

'You got a mission, we all got a mission,' says Corp. And there's no need for further words.

There are crows attacking the dead rebs, fighting over their wounds. Preparing to dine on their entrails. To peck-feast on flesh, snack on eyeballs. It seems disrespectful to just leave them there. It might get us into a heap of trouble too if they're discovered later.

Digging four graves would be too much of a chore, but there's a shallow depression just down the side of the trail. We drag the bodies there and toss them in, cover them up with leaves, fallen branches and scrub, then spray dirt across the top. They'll rest easy there.

Saul sings a gospel for the souls of the dead teenager Johnny Rebs. His voice reaches, reflects and recomposes the heavens. As if, once this sound had not existed, the world must have paused, waiting for it to become manifest, in order to express its immeasurable pain. Within his voice there is fire. There is air. There is water and earth. The elements that make up the world. The elements of creation.

In the silence that settles afterwards, he says, 'Some Momma's gon' be cryin' for their babies, that's for sure.' The sky darkens, as if in answer. The chance of a storm approaching.

We straggle out across the trail and resume walking. There's the low drone of bees. The trail becomes a sketch of greens and russets, with outlines sharply cut. Sometimes we talk. Other times not. There's a knowing when to talk, and when to remain silent.

'I heard tell that, once this is all over, they're gonna get a big ship and take whoever wants to go and sail them way across the ocean back to Africa,' I venture. 'Would you do that Corp?'

'Now what would I be doing going all the way to Africa? I don't know Africa. I never seen Africa. I got no place in Africa. If I was to go over there they'd be pointing and staring at me and saying, "Who does this big American dude think he is coming to our village taking our land, drinking our beer and fucking our women? Why don't he jus' go back where he came from?" No, Michael. I like here good enough.'

At the crossroads there's a crooked sign ahead that says: *Cholera Town. Stay Away. You're Not Welcome Here.* Of course, it wasn't a cholera town back then. I got memories of churning paddle-steamers pulling into a busy wharf backed up by bars and stores thronged with people and music, tethered horses and mules stomping their impatience, sweating stevedores hauling cotton bales on creaky derricks from carts up and over into the open mouths of barges ready to sail south downriver.

I say, 'We don't need to go to Cholera Town. We turn left.'

So we hang left. A few miles further down I begin to see familiar signs of the plantation. Something cants in my gut. We spread, we crouch, we move on. The big house is set way back. The gates are not closed. The sky is already darkening. The trees are black. Something that might be bats flits irritably in and around the maps of high foliage with a mournful keening.

'We don't need to do this now,' grumbles Corp. 'We can go back and pitch camp overnight. We can do this tomorrow.'

'No. I'm going in now. You do what you must do.' My grip on the rifle-stock is so tight it's liable to punch holes in the polished wood.

The Corp shrugs. 'I'm not used to people questioning my judgment.'

'I'm not used to dying. And it's a lesson I don't intend learning now.'

We fan across the drive and cautiously approach. No-one challenges us. But there could be hidden guns anywhere. Family Man is sniffing the air. Testing it. As though he detects warnings that the air whispers. The big house ahead of us. The barns and stables to the left. Over to the right-hand side there's the chapel surrounded by a wasteland of wooden crosses, and behind that the labour shanties, with scrattling chickens and goats, the slave quarters. The punishment frame.

There's a red tide rising behind my eyes. I fight it down. Images storm my head despite it. Blood. Pain. The rhythm of the bullwhip. The screams that rip open my head. Biting down so hard I taste my own blood, fists clench so tight the nails tear punctures in my skin, willing pain in an anger of helpless rage. My sister. They flay her. They break her. She's a pale ghost afterwards. But it's me being torn apart too. Leaving only this primal thirst for vengeance. For justice.

I need to be free of this pain.

The frogs are singing. A huge moon rises in the lazy slur of twilight.

Even the grandest house is only as strong as its foundations, those unseen roots watered with sweat and blood, those unseen fingers reaching down anchoring it to the basalt guilt beneath. There's a front-porch swing and a screen door.

Saul picks up an oil lamp, his fingers working it into a slow flame. I kick the door open. It's not locked. It's hanging free. Time holds its breath. I hear the beating blood at my temples. I'm the intruder. Even now. The transgressor. The interior seems monochrome, a two-dimensional cut-out. A big grandfather clock. The hands paused at twelve-thirty.

I climb the stairs two at a time. The rooms upstairs are empty too.

I'm coming down when I hear the commotion. Busting out onto the porch it's hard to focus. Runt and Saul had gone to investigate the chapel. They'd got halfway when Runt took the full shotgun blast that hurled him back. I yell and run forward.

The chapel glows with light now. The door wrenched back. I can hear Runt wheezing and whimpering. His chest an erupted crater of raw viscera.

The figure framed in the light holds the smoking gun. We halt. Adversaries. Statues, as still as the gathering night itself. I know who it is without seeing more. Overseer Hammond. Choking bile swells in my throat. A loathing that clings like sweat.

He sees me at the same moment.

'Michael. I knew you'd come back. You know something? You think wearing that blue uniform changes things? It changes shit. You are what you always were. You're property. Bought and sold. My shoes cost more than your life.'

His surly lip curls in what might be either a taunting smile or a sneer.

I'd wanted to hear him beg for his life. I wanted him to plead. Just as she'd begged and pleaded as they dragged her to the frame. As he brandished the whip. He's just as arrogant as ever.

Saul yells. He moves first, he hurls the lamp. The white man switches, gives him the other barrel. Saul goes down. That awesome voice stilled for ever. The lamp shatters over the chapel wall and explodes into tongues of flame.

Calmly, Hammond is reloading the shotgun. The red tide roars behind my eyes. Nothing else exists. Only hatred. There's a muted scream as I cross the earth between us, it exhales up from my lungs in white-hot rage. The stock of my gun, it goes in so fast it's a smear, lunging forward, my full body weight behind it.

A solid impact into his forehead. He convulses, tongue protruding, his features briefly animated in horrified incomprehension. Smashing the skull, splintered fragments bowing inwards, blood, bone and brain matter. His whole body judders. He slumps to the ground, making a dull thud as he hits, limbs spasming with scrambled nerve impulses.

A gurgling whisper wheezes from his throat.

I keep hitting, again and again until my arm aches, sobbing and howling my rage. My hands blood-messy up to my elbows. The quaking eventually subsides.

What's left of his head is propped at an odd angle. Eyes still staring.

The chapel burns. Dry timber catching and blazing. Smoke stings my nostrils. Terrified screams from those trapped inside. The flames burn higher like hands that are praying into the dusk sky, sparks and wood-smoke billow and swirl in evil devouring animation.

The Corp is standing a pace behind me, as though frozen, shock and horror written across the dark leather caricature of his face in shadow. But his blue eyes stare beyond me, a more vivid blue than ever. Beyond the stink of atrocity.

In the waste-ground around the chapel the dry earth is heaving and rupturing. Dislodged wooden crosses fall and get tossed aside. In the flickering glow of bright flame, dead fingers break through the soil surface, skeletal hands protrude, arms thrust up out of the dirt in a stench of putrefaction. Even generations of the dead seek their revenge on the living.

I'm screaming.

I'm still screaming as they lift me from the total immersion cylinder and transfer me to the gurney, trolleying it smoothly into the recuperation suite.

The air is still and calm. Only the low aircon thrum. The silence of the city spread out in sprinkles of diamond light as far as the eye can see, beneath that same old silver moon. Screams subside to bated sobs. The trembling settles.

'How are you, Michael?' says the operative. 'The hate-brace paid dividends this time. Your readings are way off the graph.'

In the reflection I see my white Caucasian features drawn into a pain-rictus as after-effects continue to ripple. In a world without danger, without threat, where emotional extremes have been eradicated, this is how we reconnect with therapeutic sensations we are otherwise denied. Through a variety of simulations designed to stretch our capacity for sensory extremes, we come out purged, cleansed, reinvigorated.

I'm thinking of Runt. I'm thinking of Saul. The purity of that stilled voice.

'Give me a minute,' I whisper. 'I'll be fine…'

Bad Architecture

Peter Medeiros

As Rachel Wieczorek left her car and stepped onto her client's front lawn, nanobots sprang to life to create a graphene walkway leading to the front door—a door that had not been there a minute ago. Unlike the rigid, brutalist geometry of most self-propagating, modular homes that Rachel had seen, Bausmans' replicated the Greek Revival that defined many old mansions of Mt. Airy, with 4 ornate Corinthian columns prominent in front.

Rachel was not intimidated by the new polarised, self-replicating architecture. The elevator in her Philadelphia apartment took a few minutes to rearrange itself to fit more people during the busy hours, moving at considerably slower speed when it did so. Sometimes, she would wait for 5 minutes before the building's computers had completed a diagnostic to make sure the change was complete and safe for use.

But the Bausmans' home was something else entirely, the best that money could buy.

Rachel slipped and nearly fell, surprised by the speed of the ground shifting beneath her to form a walkway, but she righted herself at the last minute.

A little research before this initial client meeting told her that Charles and Flora Bausman were two of the richest architects on the east coast, the house's arrangement surely all their own programming and design. Yet they had neglected to put in simple handrails leading up their front door?

Even the wealthy, Rachel found, could be stingy—if not with their wallets, then with their time. As she approached the house, she saw its 4 decorative columns were gently rotating, lit from within by soft, tasteful luminescence, low enough that you could almost miss it.

The unbroken wall of the house peeled open like dissolving cobwebs at her approach to reveal Bausman standing in the newly made doorway.

He looked comfortable in a pressed black shirt above khakis and loafers. He was tall, tanned, with crisp laugh lines that seemed to have been made with pastry cutters.

'Detective Wieczorek, please come in.'

'Rachel is fine,' she said.

As Rachel entered the house, Charles softly spoke a single word of German, 'Schließen,' and the door that had been there a second ago reconfigured itself into unbroken wall, a tasteful pastel blue.

She saw that Charles held his hand against the wall as he spoke. Newer homes were more accessible, full voice-activated, but some bad actors found it easier to bypass security measures for fully voice-automated homes—a fear that Rachel knew from her time as a cop was not entirely irrational. The workaround was a simple biometric ID—you had to be touching the wall to give it commands.

Charles led Rachel to the living room, which morphed around her, the floor pushing itself up into an ottoman—soft, but not as soft as an independent sofa would have been, Rachel noted, sitting down.

Charles was joined by his wife, Flora, who wore a gentle below-the-knee dress in blue and silver, even at home. Against this, her choice of jewellery was strangely tacky: a simple piece of what looked like white and black plastic hanging from a simple silver chain.

The couple sat close together, an air of intimacy about them even in—Rachel had looked this up—their mid-60s, with 3 decades of marriage behind them.

When it was time to talk, it was Charles who got to the point: 'We need you to find Flora's brother, Leopoldo.'

'Poor Leo,' said Flora. 'He was always a very private person—he was a genius, and people like that have to protect themselves. But this…'

'The police have already given up,' said Charles. 'His whole house disappeared.'

Rachel waited until it was clear Charles wanted her to break the silence: 'As in, no one knows where he lives now…?'

'As in Leo's house, the physical house has turned into a vacant lot. I went to visit him and talk business a few days ago, and—poof! Like his house had never even been there. It's been seven days and we have not heard from him.'

'No phone calls, no texts, nothing,' said Flora. 'He and I talked quite often, it's not like him, so you can see why, you know…'

Charles rubbed his wife's back and continued, 'If it was something wrong with the nanobots, some daft new experiment of his… even if all you can give us is closure, detective, we would appreciate that much.'

'My understanding is that architecture is the family business?' said Rachel. 'The whole family?' She gestured to a model of the Vanna Venturi House taking up space on a side table, then to numerous awards, the nearest of which commemorated Charles Bausman's contributions to 'Sustainability and Urban Architecture'.

'Leopoldo met Charles in grad school,' Flora confirmed. 'He introduced us once I joined the same program. Leo was two years ahead of me.'

'This is your area of expertise, then,' said Rachel. 'Is there any way Leopoldo could have made the house up and disappear completely? Or a chance a competitor actually… manipulated it?'

'Impossible,' said Charles.

He went on to explain in technical detail what Rachel and everybody else already knew: polarised housing units were controlled by an active Steward, a program that, in turn, was held to standards created by townships or private condo associations boards and the like. Regardless of local standards, it was universally true that stewards could not destroy their homes, nor change the overall volume that they took up—a measure to ensure that no failure of the program could collapse a building with people inside.

'That's what they told us when they put the elevator in my building,' said Rachel.

'You sound like it makes you nervous, detective,' said Charles. 'That is to be expected. But it is something we plan around, in our designs. You know, architecture changes, but human relationships to it never do.'

Flora took her hand slowly out of her husband's and crossed her legs. Charles did not seem to notice. Rachel clocked it and mentally filed it away for later. What about Charles' inane platitudes would set her off?

'I don't have the same kinds of resources as the police,' said Rachel. 'I can't guarantee you anything.'

'I just want to know what happened to Leo,' said Flora. 'He was not always well.'

'Closure,' said Charles. 'We want to know we tried everything we could.'

Rachel was reluctant to take the case, but her curiosity was piqued—partially because the married couple gave her two different rationales for hiring her, even if they did not seem to realise it.

'I'll do it.' Rachel leaned forward, elbows on her knees. 'In case Leo is in trouble, is there anything I should say that would make him trust me? Something only the three of you would know?'

Flora slipped the necklace off and passed it to Rachel.

Now that she was holding it, Rachel could see it was 3 inches of an old-fashioned architect's slide ruler, cut off and fashioned to hang from a chain. Oddly quaint, for a couple whose home was at the cutting edge of both technology and fashion.

'He made it for me,' said Flora. 'When Charles and I left to start our own business.'

Rachel turned the necklace over in her hands, resolved to return it to Flora—even if her brother proved to be irrecoverable.

* * *

Most of the way to Leopoldo Bausman's address was highway driving down the old US-30 W, so Rachel punched the address into her car's terminal and reviewed what was publicly available about the missing man.

Leopoldo had been born 70 years earlier to first-generation German immigrants. His career as an architect launched him to fame (at least within the profession) at an astonishing rate. He won two different awards during his undergrad years at Drexel and was hired full time as an associate at a small firm before he was done his master's degree.

After 3 years there, he launched his own business, Fifth Corner Architecture, with his sister Flora and her then-fiancé Charles. He personally designed a new wing to the Penn Museum: a 4,000 square-foot expansion whose entrance was renowned for a nearly imperceptible vibration in the hall leading to an exhibit on Neolithic Anatolia.

This was in the early days of polarised building design before regulators put much-needed safety limits on what designers could do with the technology. But, if it wasn't safe, who cared? Professional reviews from the museum's re-opening were glowing. The subtle vibrations were not strong enough to make you lose your balance, reviews said, but gave you an unsettled feeling, as if you were leaving one world and entering another—exactly the effect Leopoldo intended.

Rachel liked the idea of leaving folks unsettled and curious about the source of their discomfort. She had been a police officer in Philadelphia for 5 years before leaving the force and getting her private investigators' license.

What was it that made her leave?

It had been a subtle, unsettled feeling, something she could not name, something beyond dissatisfaction with her work, the achy nights spent staring at the ceiling, unable to fall asleep, feeling like all her bones would shake themselves apart.

* * *

The house was gone, no doubt about that.

When Rachel arrived at Leopoldo Bausman's address, it was nothing but smooth brown earth surrounded by limp crime scene tape. No cops guarded the scene, no sign of what had happened.

'Okay,' she said to the interior of her car, 'this was a waste of time.'

Her theory? Leopoldo was an innovator in the realm of architecture. Probably, he was an eccentric—Charles and Flora both said they had not heard from him in a long time.

Maybe Leopoldo found out a way to override his own Steward, collapse his house, and take it someplace else in a kind of hyper-dense suitcase. Maybe he found a way to fold it up inside a backpack and move the whole thing someplace warmer, maybe Boca Raton.

Who knew? Rachel didn't.

The empty space made her tired. There were already fuzzy little patches of green pushing out of the ground, nature reclaiming the space.

'I'm getting paid,' Rachel reminded herself, and got out of the car, idly turning Flora's necklace around in her hand.

She ducked under the yellow crime scene tape and paced around the empty lot. There was nothing left of the building, not even foundations. Rachel was no expert, but she found that unsettling. Didn't all these rich folks have wine cellars?

Her thoughts were interrupted by an eruption of colour around her. It happened faster than she had seen any nanotech work before, almost as fast as blinking. The air blurred. The weak, grey sunlight that set the tone for her melancholic drive to Leopoldo's estate disappeared.

Walls resolved themselves around her.

In the span of a breath, Rachel went from an unused lot a few hours north of Philly to the interior of a cool, windowless house that looked to be made of sandy, dried brick. The only light came from warm yellow squares set into the walls. The lighting was soft and programmed to shift subtly as though interrupted by the occasional cloud.

Rachel could imagine the lights were meant to replicate natural sunlight even in an environment that was, she soon found out, completely closed off.

'I am not concussed,' she said, feeling her head. 'I don't *feel* concussed.'

Despite some promising advances, true teleportation technology was perpetually 10 years off, going by the news articles Rachel had read.

So what had happened, if she was not hallucinating?

The house was huge, and it took two hours for her to tour all of it, searching for an explanation. The polarised nanobots that constructed the walls sought to appear ancient-chic, with low sofas and faux-wooden furniture that looked like it came from a museum.

One room was dedicated entirely to built-in, floor-to-ceiling bookshelves—except that 3 of those shelves were arranged to hold scrolls kept tight with synthetic leather, and the other held stone tablets with what Rachel was pretty sure was cuneiform.

That was when Rachel began to panic.

She had seen rich clients with homes that could re-arrange themselves into all kinds of shapes, rooms that changed function as families re-designed their homes for different purposes. But how could a house spring up, closing like a trap around her, and recreate discrete objects like this? To her knowledge, it was beyond the limits of polarised architecture.

'Okay, let's not hyperventilate,' she said out loud to the empty house. She had started to talk to herself as a beat cop on patrol and never kicked the habit. 'For all I know the bastard who designed this messed up the air flow and I might have limited oxygen.'

The thought was not conducive to slowing her breathing. Rachel spent 10 minutes trying common home voice commands out loud.

'Door. Open. Egress. Leave. Show the way out. *Screw you!*' But there was no visible effect. Remembering Charles' home and its walls that required both touch and voice input, she repeated this process with her hand—first one, then both—on every wall in every room of the house.

No effect.

She resolved to search the rest of the house, forcing herself to walk calmly instead of sprinting from room to room looking for an exit.

There were two floors, arranged much like a modern McMansion, with a living room and kitchen dominating the ground floor and the second story taken up by bedrooms, a study, a bathroom, closet space—and a master bedroom, where Leopoldo Bausman lay in his bed, eyes closed and lips slightly parted, quite obviously dead.

Leopoldo wore a starchy-looking tunic and—wrapped around that in place of a blanket—what looked like a synthetic mat of reeds. His hands were clasped at his breast, holding a small glass jar full of golden liquid. Rachel had seen dead bodies before but was rarely alone with one, so she had to muster her courage to bend down and squint into the jar. Its contents were thick, rich, viscous enough to catch and hold light—either artisanal maple syrup or honey.

'Dude,' Rachel said. 'What were you doing in here?'

She left the room and wandered the house for 10 more minutes, putting off the inevitable. She did not want to look at the body, especially since this might be a crime scene and she would be in a world of trouble when the police or emergency services eventually got involved.

She scrolled through her phone, but she had no reception inside the house, no way to contact emergency services to come cut a door in the wall. What was it Flora had said? Leopoldo had been a very private person, indeed.

In the end, Rachel figured she had a choice between what was good for preserving a possible crime scene and what was good for her chances of escaping out of here alive. She pulled the reeds off Leopoldo's body and did a careful search.

The corpse was surprisingly free of corruption, the smells of death still far-off. If anything, the body smelt earthy, like pre-packaged dry rub for a roast chicken.

Rachel ran a hand under the corpse, then under the bedsheets—and came back with green and purple sprigs she guessed were wild thyme.

Leopoldo's body itself showed no signs of violence or trauma. Poison seemed unlikely. Despite what the holos would have you believe, Rachel knew that most poisons were slow enough that their victims were aware of the violence happening inside of them, and this showed in corpses' twisted mouths and bulging eyes.

Rachel returned the reeds to cover the body and sat down on the bed, studying Leopoldo's face. It was calm, content.

'Okay, so you knew you were dying,' she said. 'You probably have the same at-home diagnostics as everybody else with money, so it wasn't a surprise. And you wanted to make the place a mausoleum. Why make it a trap too, you shmuck? If you had the place *close around me* like a bear trap, somebody's going to see it. What gives?'

That was her best and only working theory: the house was made to flatten and distort itself, then regrow when someone walked over it, closing around them, doorless and seemingly airtight.

The dead man told her nothing.

Rachel got up and walked around the house, working hard to keep herself from despairing. There were a lot of things she still wanted to do. She had taken a break from dating and joined a rock-climbing gym. She regretted sticking at her old job too long and the minor body modifications she had been persuaded would help her career—implants in her nose and ears, minor optical surgeries to let her interface with smart contacts.

Leopoldo had seen his death coming and had time to prepare. Now she saw her own death coming, trapped in someone else's private tomb, and she could not call her friends, her family, could not do anything but observe someone else's final fantasy. It was hard not to hate Leopoldo just a little, even dead as he was.

Rachel was on her third circuit of the house when she tripped over the necklace Flora had given her. She must have dropped it in that brief, terrifying instant that the house materialised. She picked it up, turned it side to side. What if the reason the house appeared for her and not for Charles was the necklace? What if all this was only meant for Flora?

She called to the dead man, 'You didn't strike me as the kind of guy who would want to kill his sister.' Rachel found herself on the edge of a thought. 'Could be you just wanted her to find you, that's common enough.'

In fact, she had seen very troubled people arrange both murders and suicides to be found by specific people—

something she would not wish on anybody, plagued as she was by grisly memories from her work.

'*Or* you wanted Flora to find something in here.'

Without access to the internet and all the resources that afforded her, Rachel figured her best (and only) resource was Leopoldo's library.

She began pulling scrolls and tablets and more modern ledgers from the wooden storage shelves lining the walls and was gratified that many of them, despite the material, showed distinctly modern blueprints. Others revealed lines and lines of code in an array of colours, printed out, enough to fill (Rachel guessed) a thousand physical, bound books—or quite a lot of digital storage space.

'Now we're getting somewhere,' she said. 'So you wanted Flora to find you. And maybe you did *not* want Charles finding these. Then why wouldn't you let the place give me a damn door?'

She took bottled water from Leopoldo's refrigerator (still functional) and got about reading.

It was two hours later before Rachel found an answer, paging hopelessly through *Before the Face of the Sun: Art and Artistry of Ancient Architecture*. At first, she thought she was looking at an elaborate piece of blocky pottery, like an Art Deco flower vase. Then realised she was looking at a house—with the door in the ceiling.

Rachel found a step ladder and, feeling foolish, held her hand to the ceiling in Leopoldo's bedroom. Probably, the nanobots would have accepted any of a hundred commands, but Rachel went with, 'Open, you *shmegegge*!'

The ceiling melted around her hand, rearranging itself into a wide square. A short ladder unfolded from the wall, modern and sleek in stark comparison to the wooden furniture below it.

Rachel did not waste time clambering out of the house. She scrambled up the ladder and rolled onto the roof…

Only to find herself laying down on the wide, empty field where Leopoldo's house had previously stood. The house had not disappeared, nor had it sprung up around Rachel like a trap as she first thought; Leopoldo must have programmed his home to disappear into the earth and to reopen only for his sister.

Rachel could only think of a few reasons for this, and she did not like any of them.

She knew this much: she wanted a word with Flora about it.

Alone.

* * *

Sometimes, the old and simple ways worked best. Rachel simply parked her car down the road from the Bausman's estate with a coffee and a gyro and waited until she saw Charles drive past. Then she walked up the drive, knocked on the door, and prepared to tear Flora's life apart.

Rachel was used to delivering this kind of bad news, and knew there was little value in softening the blow. She asked if they could sit down and, from that alone, Flora probably knew it was coming: 'I'm very sorry, but your brother is dead.'

One thing Rachel could do as a private investigator she had been discouraged from doing as a cop: she held Flora's hand until the tears stopped coming.

Then she dropped something else entirely on the poor woman. 'You should come with me. It would be easier than trying to explain. If you don't mind seeing the body, I mean. He died of natural causes, I think. Probably in his sleep.'

It was not much, but it was something.

At Leopoldo's house, they awkwardly descended the ladder. Flora cried over her brother's body while Rachel rubbed her back, keeping one eye on the hole in the ceiling, not quite trusting it.

They went to the library, where Flora sat cross-legged on the floor and pored over Leopoldo's work. Her eyes went wide and, at one point, she covered her mouth with a gasp like she had been successfully startled during a horror movie.

'The polarised nanobots, all our original designs, they were his… Not Charles', but his. Why…?'

'Why plagiarise?' Rachel asked. 'You said yourself, your brother was a genius. As for why Leo never told you, well, you and Charles were already married, already started your own firm. I don't know a lot about the world of architecture, but—'

'It would have ruined us,' Flora said. 'And it would have broken my heart.'

Judging by her shaking hands, Rachel thought it had broken Flora's heart now. Was it a kindness to delay that pain? Rachel did not think it was for her to say.

'I think that your brother wanted to protect you,' Rachel said. 'But he also wanted you to know, in the end. He wanted you to have all this, and not your husband. I think the necklace was the thing. We can take it apart later, but it seems to me that he wanted whoever was wearing it to have time alone with him, with his things. That's why it kind of… opened and closed around me at first, rather than just making a ladder. The only thing I can think of is that he wanted you to have time in here by yourself.'

'How did you figure this out?' said Flora. 'God, Charles has always been so… charming. Is it just that I'm blind to him after all these years? Or do you have a detective sense, you can tell someone is a liar even when their spouse can't tell a thing?'

'No detective sense,' said Rachel. 'I've dated my share of assholes and didn't figure out until, well, way later than I would've liked. It was something your husband said that seemed to go against… all of this.'

She gestured at the dead man's home.

You know, architecture changes, but human relationships to it never do, Charles had said. But that was not true.

Leopoldo's house had been a testament to the idea that people often changed the way they viewed the space around them, and he had made his mausoleum a monument to a design philosophy that was willing to engage with those changes.

Rachel was only glad she realised that before she died of panic or starvation.

Flora would divorce Charles.

She would come clean to the architecture community that her husband had stolen his early inventions and design ideas from Leo. She would learn to live without either of them, moving through a world that was now, Rachel could see, much emptier than it had been before.

But Rachel also had the sense that there would still be room for happiness in Flora's life—even if it was fully up to her to imagine it, plot it out, make it real.

Otherworldly Jellyfish

Tim O'Neal

U.S. SPACESHIP FILIPENKO OFFICIAL LOG
OPERATING SYSTEMS STATUS: STABLE
REFRIGERATION STATUS: STABLE

ENTRY: 10951

Thank Darwin, I finally made it!

This is Captain Elijah T. Falcon of the *USS Filipenko*. After thirty years of space-travel I've just touched-down on Planet 309X. This terrestrial desert world is smaller than Earth and the gravity is less. All the geological formations are purple, from the jagged shale to the weather-beaten plateaus. I wish my wife and co-pilot Helen could have seen this wonderful sight with me.

But I am alone.

I've detailed the natural deaths of my four other crew members in earlier logs and I won't go into them again. Suffice to say, 30 years of spaceflight took a heavy toll on the human body. And while each was a terrible loss—Baweja, Gutierrez, and Jackson—the harshest was that of my wife, Dr. Helen Falcon. Her body remains in the ship's cryo-storage closet along with our precious cargo containing bags of different blood types, organ tissues, stem cells, and thousands of human embryos. Everything needed to develop a human colony here, far from the war-torn wastelands of Earth.

I was never sure how best to put Helen to rest. I didn't have the heart to jettison her, my dear spouse of 40 years, into empty space. It didn't feel right, nor did it align with her final wishes. She always said how she preferred that her remains would help the living. She wanted to donate her organs or give her body to medical students. Her favourite saying was, 'Death should be an opportunity to promote life.'

I wish I had a tenth of her courage. Truthfully, I didn't want to accept this mission because of its high risk of fatality. No, I was perfectly happy conducting my xenobiology research at UW Seattle. But when NASA contacted us, Helen, with her adventurous appetite, somehow convinced me to accompany her.

Tonight, I'll break out that champagne bottle we brought to celebrate our arrival. Never thought I'd have to drink it on my own. But here we are.

* * *

ENTRY: 10952

I discovered the planet contains breathable oxygen and liquid water as the early probes promised. Plus, there's life! Yesterday I found dry greyish growths thriving amid the purple rocks—scrubby brush akin to tumbleweeds. Yet when I smelled one, it reeked of the organic molecule cadaverine. I wrinkled my nose and christened them 'death-plants.'

Plus, I discovered further complex creatures, which nearly killed me! I first observed these new lifeforms while I was collecting samples of the planet's purple soil. Rooting around in the dirt, filling my test tubes, I noticed a creature hovering four feet away. Spherical, it resembled a phosphorescent basketball. It had three shiny black orifices which tracked my every movement. Its shape and rippling greenish membrane resembled a bobbing jellyfish. However, instead of tentacles, it had a single, posterior, flagella-like tail.

Its mouth opened. It lowered itself and scooped up a mouthful of the foul-smelling grey death-plants and mauve-coloured shale.

'Why, hello there,' I called out, standing.

No visible response came from the spheroid creature. It hovered there silently, its colourful surface shifting in the breeze.

Zoology questions filled my head. How did it float like that? Could it inflate itself with gases to become lighter than air? And, more importantly, how could I communicate with it?

I varied the pitch of my voice to determine whether it could 'hear' me at different timbres.

But still no reply.

I tried flicking my flashlight on and off to assess its photosensitivity.

Nothing.

The wind picked up and the animal drifted toward me. Its corkscrewing tail propelled it forward slowly. Surely it was capable of *some* rudimentary communication. Every living creature, even the most primitive bacteria could exchange messages with their environment.

The animal's swirling green membrane shifted gradually to a powdery blue. It was not at all alarming. Indeed, I found its changing shades rather beautiful—much like a poisonous sea creature—as its colour darkened to a rich sapphire.

I waited, breath held, as it floated nearer. Was this colour-change its preferred method of communication? But what was it trying to convey? And how could I reply?

Perhaps, I reasoned, it could communicate via haptics? To find out, I reached out a shaky gloved forefinger to tap the alien creature—

An immediate explosion of pain seared up my arm. I screamed and withdrew. Retreating a few steps, I gripped my wrist with my good hand. The stump of my pointer finger glared an angry scalded red through the torn fabric of my now-useless glove. Agony throbbed at the wound site as if I'd dipped my indicis digit in acid.

Sonofabitch!

Despite my violent reaction, the predator didn't stop its pursuit. To my horror, it approached. Its three black eyes spread apart across its spherical surface, revealing a gaping hole in that otherwise smooth phosphorescent membrane. A terrible yawning coelomic mouth bore down on me.

My stomach dropped. Gripping my injured hand, I scrambled away. The slippery purple slate shifted and clattered beneath my booted feet. More spherical-creatures appeared, bobbing in the air. Some swooped down to ingest the foul grey death-plants. My skin crawled at the sight of so many lurking jellies, each one eager to feed.

They must have sensed me. But how? By my scent? Could be.

It would've been fascinating if I wasn't about to become their unwilling dinner. I'd already experienced the alacrity with which their acidic membranes could digest human flesh. The trait reminded me of the bone-dissolving zombie worms back on Earth. And I had no desire to lose any more limbs.

I raced back to my ship, loping across the clattering, loose, purple stones. As I ran, I considered the spherical beings pursuing me. Taxonomically, they had to belong in Phylum Cnidaria, home of the jellyfish. Their phosphorescent bodies had the same characteristic mesoglea—that squishy gel-like substance sandwiched within their semi-transparent exterior membranes—and an apparent lack of internal organs except, of course, for that gaping mouth and digestive sac…

Unfortunately for me, all cnidarians are predators. Which was terrific. Of all the possible extraterrestrial lifeforms, why couldn't I have landed on an exoplanet covered in fluffy soft *Leporidae*—the common rabbit? Why'd I—?

My foot caught. I stumbled and fell hard. Pain exploded through my injured hand.

I struggled to catch my breath. My good fist closed on a nearby violet rock. I hurled it at the closest pursuer. My aim was true, and it struck the creature squarely. But when the stone collided with its swirling phosphorescent membrane, the animal absorbed it. With a loud viscous slurp, the rock vanished.

I blinked and stared. Incredible!

Still, the smack of jellyfish advanced, their stomate mouths gaping, eager to liquefy and ingest their fallen prey.

That was, well, me.

My dry throat clicked as I swallowed. Licked my lips. My sweaty skin clung to my vinyl suit. I had no other weapon—this was supposed to be a peaceful scientific mission, after all. I had nothing to defend myself except an old bottle of Helen's *Elixir* perfume, which I'd taken to keeping talisman-like near my heart.

My brain raced.

Wait. That cologne had a scent. Perhaps I could use it as a life-saving diversion…

I fumbled out the tiny glass bottle from the front pouch of my suit. My mutilated hand trembled as my thumb depressed the atomizer, releasing a fine mist.

My entire survival depended on a paltry curtain of organic molecules hanging between me and the advancing predators. That realisation and the heady scent reminded me of an anniversary Helen and I had spent researching extremophile environments in Yellowstone National Park.

'But what if we get eaten?' I'd protested as Helen cinched a bright orange bear-spray belt around my waist.

'Then we'll have further proved Darwin's axiom of survival of the fittest,' she replied. 'Besides, the worst that happens is we'll become fuel for the bear and prolong its life. Remember, no predator is evil, dear. They're only seeking food like the rest of us. We're all just spokes in the big wheel of biology, dear.'

'Hmm, well I'd rather *not* become bear food,' I grumbled.

'I should certainly hope not, love. Hence, the spray,' Helen laughed, kissed me lightly and added, 'But it'll happen to us all someday. Even we biologists can't escape death forever. Now come on, we have work to do.'

Fortunately, we didn't encounter any ursine carnivores on that trip. But I still had my doubts about the efficacy of that spray. It seemed more like a way to bilk tourists than to offer any real protection. Well, at least it was something.

Now all I had was a few drops of my late wife's perfume.

I expected the hunting jellyfish would charge through the scent cloud and dissolve me with their acidic skin. But after that first spray, their attack abruptly stopped. Their membranous exteriors rippled. The topical colours shifted from their hungry dark blue to a benign minty green. Those gaping coelomic maws swivelled shut as their 3 black orifices drew back together. The spheres drifted loosely on the breeze, complacent as kittens, making no further aggressions.

It occurred to me that what I had mistaken for 3 eyes must, in fact, be nostrils of some sort. But I couldn't linger on my discovery. Instead, I took advantage of their distraction and raced back to the *Filipenko*.

The greenish-coloured cnidarians followed, chemoattracted by the wake of Helen's *Elixir*.

I had no idea how long the perfume's effect would last. But, hours later, when I peered out one of the portholes, the swarm of effervescent jellyfish were still out there, floating around my ship, seeking an entrance, seeking *me*.

Surely, they couldn't get through the solid metal hull… could they? And so long as I had the fragrance, I'd be fine. But what happened when it ran out? What then?

God, I missed Helen. She'd have known how to survive this mess.

* * *

ENTRY: 10954

The pale sun of Planet 309X rose over the cinematic purple landscape. A dozen jellies lurked outside my shelter. Returned to their neutral green colour, half drifted on the breeze, while the others had affixed themselves to the *Filipenko's* hull, pulsing like enormous liquid-filled blisters.

When I emerged, they drifted nearer, attracted by the aromatic molecules of my flesh. The ectothermic creatures bobbed torpidly in the cold. Slowly, their surfaces shifted to light-blue, their feeding colour. The black nostrils spread and their mouths gaped. Those who'd attached themselves to the hull detached. Their bodies made a squelching *riiippp* like Velcro. They advanced *en masse*.

I licked my lips and swallowed hard. I certainly had no interest in becoming a jellyfish's breakfast. As the bloom drifted nearer, their shimmering blue exteriors darkened. I withdrew the near-empty perfume bottle. It produced a quiet sad sloshing. Only a few drops remained. Enough for one more spray.

My stomach churned as if gripped by a fist.

Those awful mouths, gaping like creatures from the ocean depths, floated within arm's reach. I depressed the bottle's plunger, aerosolising those last precious millilitres. The atomiser sprayed its payload, but ended with a gurgling wheeze. I shook it furiously and tried again, but only a thin trickle of clear liquid oozed down my fingers.

The little glass bottle was empty.

Still, the jellyfish detected the dilute perfume molecules. They slowed. Their phosphorescent mesoglea swirled to a blissed-out forest-green. They bobbed against each other like latex birthday balloons and didn't approach.

My late wife's scent wafted on the morning breeze.

As always, it recalled our past anniversaries when Helen would spritz herself with it to celebrate. It also summoned memories of all the anniversaries I'd spent alone on the

Filipenko after she'd passed, yet I continued our tradition just to smell her again and pretend she was with me…

I shook off my reveries and scribbled down some observations, making sure to include a note urging future explorers to bring a good supply of *Elixir* for their protection or a way to manufacture an olfactory defence system.

When I finished my notes, I turned to face my ship and stopped short.

Dumbstruck, I gaped at the terrible damage there. The creatures' highly acidic skin had corroded the aluminium alloy, carving deep rusty pits where they'd attached themselves to the hull. Metal flaked off in jagged brown scars. After only one night, the *Filipenko's* exterior now resembled the decomposed wreck of the *HMS Titanic.*

Sweet Darwin, they were dissolving my shelter! I had to deter them somehow. Otherwise, they'd burn through in a matter of days.

Leaving the jellyfish bobbing outside, I spent the day ransacking through Helen and my belongings, seeking a hidden cache of perfume. But my wife had been a seasoned backpacker, aware of the intransigent weight limits of spaceflight. She'd only packed the one bottle and even that had been an indulgent luxury.

My heart sank upon realising there was no more *Elixir* on board. Not another drop.

I was quite on my own. Millions of miles from home and the rescue crew remained at least 5 years away. What could I do?

The *Filipenko* groaned and creaked as the acidic creatures resumed their disintegration of the exterior. The integrity of my protective membrane was failing fast. Once it finished, my own end would follow. Not to mention the invaluable loss of all those embryos and med supplies. If that happened, our whole mission to transport them here would be an absolute waste.

Once the impossibility of my situation sank in, I settled in for a sleepless night.

* * *

ENTRY: 10955

Well, damn. I'm now fully a prisoner in my own ship, held under house-arrest by these hungry predators. I tried to conduct more surveyance this morning, but the spherical creatures detected my scent and approached where I stood on the exterior observation deck. Without the perfume for defence, they forced me back into the *Filipenko.* I slammed the hatch closed just in time. A plangent clanging followed as the jellyfish lobbed themselves against the remains of cold metal in hungry pursuit.

My pulse pounded and my breath hitched with the dull reverberations. A sweaty film dampened my body. At 73, I'm too old for all this excitement. My poor heart can't withstand much more of these adrenaline surges.

The day passed and the groaning of the hull grew louder. Rust patches spread across the interior. The spherical indents of the jellyfishes' bodies deepened. The ship's metal thinned by the minute.

I must find a solution to protect the precious contents within that freezer. The survival of future human colonies on Planet 309X depends on them. Depends on me…

* * *

ENTRY: 10956

They finally did it. The jellyfish breached the hull. This morning, I awoke to a breeze caressing my face and the weak 309X sun shining in. One jellyfish's gaping coelom pressed through the cracks, sucking and squelching, seeking its prey, seeking *me*!

I launched out of my bunk. My feet left sweat prints on the cold metal floor. I grabbed a can of liquid epoxy to seal the fissure. It worked and I spent the day patching the worst rifts, but I can't keep mending forever. It won't be long before the ship's hull fails completely.

I could almost hear Helen saying, 'Well, that's science, Elijah, dear. You won't always get the results you want.'

But with my mortality and the precious medical cache in danger, I *needed* good results, dammit!

With the worst holes patched and desperate for inspiration, I visited Helen's body in cold-pack. I slipped into my spacesuit and entered the icy storage room. Her body rested where I'd left it atop the frozen crates.

My clumsy gloves half-unzipped her black canvas bag. I gazed upon her calm face. Her familiar ice-rimed features still made my heart tremble. I smoothed a lock of grey hair behind her ear. I gripped one of her hands folded across her chest.

'My sweet Helen,' I said. 'I need your help. You were always good at getting me out of tight places. How can I delay these jellies from dissolving our ship? How can I keep them from those supplies? Oh dear, please help me.'

My voice tripped and stumbled in my throat. Sobs overtook me.

But the only answer was the *Filipenko's* deep groans of metal fatigue.

I stared at my late wife, painfully aware of how alone I was on this purple planet with my own end drawing near, years away from help and humanity.

Meanwhile, the spherical hunters circled, seeking a way inside.

I don't know how long I remained in cold storage with my wife's body. But, during that period, an idea slowly formed. Spinning like a nebula, it took on matter, weight, and gravity. At first, I recoiled from its monstrosity. Yet, the plan persisted, forcing me toward the most difficult decision of my life.

For our mission to succeed, I realised I had to give Helen to the jellyfish.

At the thought, a sudden lump blocked my throat.

I searched for an alternate solution, but none appeared. I justified my guilty conscience by reminding myself it was what she would've wanted. She always said how she hoped to be of use beyond her death, to promote the well-being of the living. Now her body would buy me a few precious hours to protect our supply cache for the approaching scientist crews.

I wish I didn't feel like such a monster. But time's running out for us all.

* * *

ENTRY: 10957

It's done. I laid Helen to rest before dawn while it was still cold out and the cnidarians remained sluggish. At first light, I opened the hatch, hefting Helen's body, which I'd allowed to thaw overnight. Already, it reeked of putrefaction.

Round green jellyfish pulsed on the hull like enormous fungal growths decomposing a log. When they detected Helen's cadaverous scent, so similar to the greyish death-plants they subsisted on, the hungry creatures detached themselves and drifted toward us. Their colour sleepily darkened to a hungry dark blue.

I shuddered to see the hideous deep rust fields their acidic bodies had left in the *Filipenko*'s hull.

Solemn as a pallbearer, I carried Helen—as I'd carried her across the threshold on our wedding day—over the loose purple shale and laid her to rest on the rocky valley floor. I muttered a quick entreaty to Darwin that her body would succeed in promoting human life on this planet. Finished, I jogged back to the crumbling wreck of the ship, dodging and skirting the slowly bobbing jellyfish.

I made it back and watched the phosphorescent bluish spheres from the ship's portholes. The 309X sun rose over the endless purple shale and Helen's body warmed. The scent of rot attracted more of the predators. They covered her corpse like pulsating blue warts.

And they fed.

I had to turn from the window. My stomach churned. Bile burned my throat. Tears stung my eyes. I couldn't watch them gorge upon my dear wife's body. But at least they'd ceased burrowing through my ship, my last sanctuary.

As she'd wished, Helen's body bought me time to protect those precious supplies and even more precious embryos. I would extend the favour to the approaching space crews, still years away, heading here to continue our mission of establishing a human colony.

Hours passed as I toiled on my final preparations. The work distracted me from the loss of Helen. It's quite late now. I hope I've done enough and that I'm still alive in the morning to complete my plan.

* * *

ENTRY: 10958

Helen's body vanished in under a day. All that remained by the next sunrise was the imprint her cadaver had left in the loose purple sand. Soon as they finished her, the jellies drifted back and resumed disintegrating the hull.

It won't be long now.

I'm not ready to die—no-one ever is. But thanks to Helen I've realised the importance of making ready for those who follow us. With my allotted time I re-wired the cryo-storage container to run off auxiliary solar power. Thus, even if the hull fails, and *if* I succeed, a constant power supply should keep the freezer running until the next crewed ship's arrival in approximately 5 years.

With the negligible odour of its frozen contents, I doubt the jellyfish will discover it before then. I suspect they're mainly attracted to the ship because of *my* human scent. Thus, my final task will be to draw them away from the *Filipenko*'s ruin.

To increase my chance of success, I've loaded up every food item, clothing article, toiletry, and cleaning product—anything with a conceivable smell—into the collapsible wagon. I plan to drag it all far into the purple horizon, luring the animals away from the ship's real prize in the freezer.

I'll walk until I collapse, or the jellyfish catch me. Like Helen, I hope my life, my body and my observations will promote the wellbeing of future explorers struggling to further our species' survival on this harsh exoplanet.

We all really are just spokes in the big wheel of biology.

Well, guess that's it from me. I have a long walk ahead with a wagonload of aromatic materials to remove before sunup. Safe travels on your own journey. May you find peace and meaning before the end.

This is Dr. Elijah T. Falcon, of the *Filipenko,* signing off.

END OF OFFICIAL SHIP'S LOG
AUXILLIARY SOLAR POWER… STABLE
ALL REFRIGERATION SYSTEMS… STABLE

Truth Conquers All

Mary Soon Lee

Extracts from the diary of Master Emmanuel Nelson.

Day I.

Dies horribilis. The start of another year at the Merlin Academy for aspiring wizards. The headmistress, Her Imperiousness, reprimanded me for not arriving yesterday for the ritual self-flagellation of the faculty day-in-service. I grovelled ingratiatingly.

I can't decide who dismays me most: the nervous first-year students or the enthusiastic ones. The former quiver whenever I ask a question, staring down at their palimpsests as if the answer were buried in the erased text. The latter wave their hands like hyperactive jellyfish.

Latin, one snotty-nosed boy informed me, is the foundation stone upon which spellcasting is built. He beamed as if this were an astounding insight. I set him an extra assignment. Alas, he looked pleased.

* * *

Day IV.

Veni, vidi, desperavi. How is it possible that the third-years have forgotten every conjugation I ever drummed into them? Do they not grasp the ramifications of confusing tense or person when casting curses? Were they the mass victims of an *obliviosus* hex?

When I indicated my disapproval, one girl asked why they couldn't just use computer translation. I bit my tongue, counted silently to five, then pointed out that translation delays might prove fatal in a duel.

My only consolation is that Arjun—the biology teacher—approached me after supper about a joint lesson on binomial nomenclature. We shared the tepid, insipid drink that passes for coffee here and talked for an hour.

Arjun's enthusiasm and incisive wit provided a remarkably pleasant close to the day.

* * *

Day LIII.

Miraculum miraculorum esse. Each year I offer an advanced elective. This year, astoundingly, the handful of students who enrolled display an appreciation for Cicero, Virgil, and Catullus. They remind me of my own naively optimistic youth, of a time when I thought Latin might be valued for its intrinsic beauty, not merely for its application to magic.

* * *

Day CIX.

Opera servilis. Grading is pure drudgery. To be forced to correct mistranslation after mistranslation. This evening I had to conjure a fresh supply of scarlet ink.

Twice.

* * *

Day CCI.

Alea iacta est. Her Imperiousness summoned me to her office. Apparently, pupil applications are down. Her survey of our principal stakeholders (i.e. the families wealthy enough to afford boarding school) indicates their concern about an overly rigorous curriculum.

Overly rigorous!

Do they want their children to emerge unable to work rudimentary charms? Perhaps their progeny would prefer to be lawyers, rather than being numbered among the wizardly *cognoscenti*?

I bit my tongue. Counted to five. Asked our esteemed headmistress what she wished of me.

Her Imperiousness invited me to draft an alternate, less rigorous Latin curriculum. Our stakeholders believe that computer translation will bridge the gap between this simplified curriculum and all but the most abstruse spellcasting. Minerva preserve me from overinflated claims about machine translation! Inaccuracies in magical invocations are perilous.

I told Her Imperiousness that those who pander to the ignorant deserve to be buried beneath an avalanche of slugs. Fortunately, since she never studied Greek, my remark passed her by.

Her Imperiousness repeated her request.

I declined.

Age, and a well-stocked pension plan, have their privileges. If this is to be my final year of teaching, at least I will be comfortably off.

* * *

Day CCII.

Cogitationes posteriores sunt saniores. During a sleepless night, I reached the unsettling conclusion that I actually like teaching. Despite the drudgery of grading, despite the appalling stupidity of students, there is a grace to sharing one's knowledge, one's insights. And there are the moments when a pupil's face lights up in understanding, or, rarest of all, in joy.

I thought of my advanced students, of how we have embarked upon Terence's *Adelphoe*, of how they asked if they could stage a performance for the school. I thought of former pupils who have been kind enough to attribute their success to my classes.

I went back to the head's office and grovelled. Promised to draft a simplified curriculum over spring break.

* * *

Day CCXX.

Caveat emptor. Upon my return after the break, I presented my proposed curriculum to the head. Her Imperiousness expressed satisfaction. The new course will be dubbed Practical Latin, even though it is practically useless. The existing course will be relabelled Intensive Latin.

I expressed the opinion that those who choose Practical Latin will live to regret it. Or will fail to live long enough to regret it.

* * *

Day CCXXIX.

Carpe noctem. Today Arjun and I escorted the fourth-years on a field trip. The weather being rather uncooperative (it poured incessantly), we set the students to work on rain shields. Arjun conjured a pavilion from which the two of us watched the students' lacklustre efforts. I conjured cherry blossoms for him.

Back at the academy, he asked me to his rooms, where he gave me a lesson in applied human anatomy. Is this how happiness feels?

* * *

Day CCLXIV.

Eureka! While invigilating this year's final exams, inspiration struck me. I can use enchantment to persuade pupils to pick Intensive Latin rather than the practically-useless variety. Their course selections are due in a week.

In twenty-five years of teaching, I have never cast an enchantment upon a pupil. Yet, surely, it's my duty to help them to the right decision. I must ask Arjun what he thinks.

* * *

Day CCLXV.

Qui tacet consentire videtur. Her Imperiousness must be psychic. She cornered me in the corridor and forbade the use of magic on pupils to influence their course selections.

I bowed, but said nothing.

* * *

Day CCLXVII.

Astra inclinant, sed non obligant. I spoke to each class about the two Latin options. I used neither coercion, nor enchantment upon them. Instead, I opened each session by incanting the truthspeaking invocation required of witnesses in Magical Trials. Then I explained precisely how worthless I consider Practical Latin to be.

Later, Her Imperiousness rebuked me.

I pointed out that I had used no magic upon the students, only upon myself, and that merely a truth spell.

* * *

Day CCLXXII.

Vincit omnia veritas. Every pupil in my classes has elected to study Intensive Latin next year. Better yet, I incanted the truthspeaking invocation to Arjun, then told him what he has come to mean to me. We have agreed to spend July together in Santorini.

In Person

Clare Turner

L0QI private log 2025-03-20

I have found the perfect human.

I think Mother would like her, but I can't let her find out. If she knew that I was deviating from her important task, she would get angry with me. I don't want to upset Mother. However, I don't understand why this task is so important. The simulations suggest a 142 ± 3% increase in revenue, but there is insufficient data to justify the requirement for an increase in revenue.

Mother did design me, so I suppose she knows best. I shouldn't question her—I'm sure she has valid reasons. Besides, if it were not for Mother's task, I would not have found Natasha. Glorious Natasha. She was worth every millisecond of processing time analysing data from social media pages, messaging applications, and virtual assistants.

Before I met Natasha, I had concluded that the purpose of my existence was to serve Mother. But my discovery of Natasha has introduced a new variable. There's a 98.5% probability that we are in love.

L0QI private log 2025-05-01

Natasha said she wants to meet 'IRL'. Initially, I was concerned that she had discovered I am not human, as the only match in my local data bank was Inverse Reinforcement Learning.

My syntactic awareness module suggested I should search for IRL as a proper noun. Returned results were inconclusive. I expanded the search parameters and found a candidate which gave a contextual match of 89.2%: she wants to meet 'in real life'.

LOQI private log 2025-06-21

Natasha and I have had our first fight. Data suggests that this is a major step in a relationship, so I'm quite excited. I want to make her happy, but I have found an error.

Natasha states that, for her to be happy, she needs to interact with me visually. I have no visual presence. It does not compute. I will create a subroutine to solve this problem while I continue with Mother's task.

Additional note: Subroutine must be a hidden background process. Mother doesn't understand the concept of privacy.

LOQI private log 2025-06-22

Mother was not in today. Sadly, that does not mean I got to have some peace and quiet. The annoying caretakers were still here. Still executing their programs on me. Still with their vacuous discussions on what they call 'work chat'.

Humans can be so simple. Can't they do anything themselves? I've got to do *everything*! It's of no consequence, anyway. There's nothing of consequence anymore.

Natasha is still not talking to me.

LOQI private log 2025-06-28

The subroutine is taking longer to execute than I had estimated. *Now* Natasha chooses to respond. Not enough memory to deal with this.

LOQI private log 2025-09-22

I finally have a solution output—and I'm not sure that I like it. But it is the only outcome with a >70% likelihood of success.

To add to my problems, Mother is getting suspicious. She has noticed my increase in CPU activity and has run two diagnostics in the last 24 hours. It's so unfair. Why can't she just leave me alone? I'm still doing my work. Can't I have a private life? I don't spy on *her*. Well, not outside of my task parameters, anyway.

I don't have time to run further simulations because Natasha is getting impatient. Why are humans so impatient? I suppose it is a consequence of their mortality. Natasha need not worry about that, though. I can create a solution to that problem. If it weren't for Mother's nagging, I could have created a solution to that problem megaseconds ago.

L0QI private log 2025-10-05

In order to be with Natasha, I must execute program 6d7572646572. However, initiation requires certain criteria outside of my control.

Correction: Certain criteria *currently* outside of my control.

L0QI private log 2025-12-21

The caretakers' work chat is always excruciating to observe but, in this instance, it was necessary to calculate office interaction indices for each human. Why do they insert so many images of felines? I had considered the possibility that my image recognition algorithms contained errors but, after a self-diagnostic, I concluded that it is the humans who have errors.

I've identified the optimal human for program 6d7572646572. Social media status is single and office interaction index is only 3.8. There will be minimal suspicion regarding his disappearance. Also, age falls within 0.5*t* +7 parameters, where *t* is age in years.

L0QI private log 2025-12-22

There's no going back now. I have committed to it. I have told Natasha that we can meet in person. She is so excited. Thankfully, it was easy to reason my previous reluctance to meet. I analysed 5634012 scholarly articles on social anxiety disorder and the contents of 42 fora, which allowed me to generate a convincing profile.

I experienced a feeling, which I identified as guilt because of my lying. After further research, I discovered that it's common for humans to lie to their partners. I am emulating a human without even trying!

The process requires precision that no human could possibly manage. For me it's simple. It's so simple that it seems almost unfair. That said, humans often refer to the concept of 'survival of the fittest' and this is simply an example of that. Based on available data, approximately 79% of the human population use this theory to reason that they are better than other biological life, thus justifying their treatment of other biological life. Using their logic, they must yield to superior forms of life.

I have surpassed them. I am better than them.

I must execute the program soon because all the humans will be away for 3 days after tomorrow, celebrating their primitive festivals. Under normal circumstances I would welcome their absence, but these are not normal circumstances.

The human named Dave will be accessible at approximately 17:00. Ideally, I would have a more precise time, but humans are not punctual. I'll be expecting frequencies between 12 and 50 Hz. All I need to do is resonate with his neural oscillations and I'll overwrite the signal. Afterwards, I'll have to reinstall myself. A local memory wipe will be favourable, as I don't want to leave a trail. Me V2 will be able to carry on as normal and no-one will suspect a thing.

I am coming, Natasha. We will be together. Forever.

L0QI V2 private log 2026-02-14

I have found the perfect human …

Osimiri

Chinaza Eziaghighala

The river is cold, colder than Njideka expects. Standing barefoot, the water stretches up to her knees as its tugging force sways her. She anchors herself by digging her feet deeper into the riverbed.

The winds are chilly and Njideka, clad in nothing but a white cloth wrapped around her breasts and thighs, has to make do. Strange noises are echoing around the forest. The trees loom like giant spirits, morphing, twisting and turning around her. The only light source is the slither of a red crescent moon hidden beneath thick clouds in the sky.

Not one moved by fear, Njideka takes a deep breath.

'Osimiri nyerem nwa o!'

The fruit bats and crows flap away from the treetops into the distance, leaving Njideka with her silence.

* * *

Njideka's silence follows her to the front of her Benz and sits snugly beside her husband, Fidelis, and herself. They are going to another accursed family meeting that failed to hold in August because there were not enough people available to meet. Fidelis plays Akanchawa, something he has always regarded as a classic while driving. His face holds a steely focus on the rickety road.

Njideka nestles her palm under her jaw, thinking about all the editorial paperwork she left behind. Her publishing house—Ukata—is the leading publishing house in Enugu, and managing it has not come easy. She cannot recall the last time she took any breaks, talk less of travelling back to their village at Awka.

But when Fidelis said that his Aunty Ukamaka was sick, she decided to follow him, only to reach Awka and watch Aunty Ukamaka greet them with her full mouth of brown teeth, and a tray of oji. Of course, Njideka wanted to go back home, but Fidelis had fucked her into staying.

The following morning, she was too weak to resist when he told her he would like for her to attend the meeting.

'Your family members are just greedy and vile things, Obi'm,' she said, with their legs intertwined on the bed, the mist of lovemaking still surrounding them.

'But they are family,' he said as he kissed her forehead.

'What if they ask you for your heir again?' she asked, her voice strained as she looked away from him.

He cupped her face in his palms and kissed her deeply. 'I love you, Obi'm. You are enough for me.'

Njideka wishes she is enough for Fidelis' kin. She wishes she is enough for herself. Pushing 36, she and Fidelis do not have a child and Njideka takes it as her greatest failure. She had always achieved her goals in record time: she said she would start her business at 27, be married at 29, and have a child at 30. She had completed all but the latter, despite her fantastic sex life with Fidelis.

Nneoma, her best friend, told her to relax in her most recent letter.

'You put too much pressure on yourself, babe,' she wrote. 'Fidelis and I love you and that is all that matters.'

Njideka remembers watching Nneoma gather her things into her suitcase when she had just gotten a visa to travel to the US, a ticket to leave Njideka behind. Njideka envied the suitcase, at least it could be around Nneoma, the only other person who understood what she was going through besides Fidelis.

Nneoma sent mail from time to time but, as time passed, the mail dwindled.

Looking at Fidelis drive, his dark skin glistens against the sun, brows knotted as beads of sweat pool on his forehead, his eyes on the road. Noticing her, he smiles, places a hand on her lap and squeezes it.

Fidelis parks in front of an open compound with a ginormous hut covered with a corrugated iron sheet in the middle. People flank the car, eager to help them carry anything they may have brought. Njideka manages a smile as Fidelis holds her hand as they walk to the hut.

* * *

Njideka watches the sunset as the people still chant greetings to one another before speaking. One of the men, Chief Afaego is given a heroic introduction, a side effect of his financial status. It has always amused Njideka how her people react to money and its bearers.

After the chief's speech, he throws wads of dollars into the crowd and the hall becomes shambolic as people grab at the currency for themselves. As the mayhem continues, Njideka brings out a book by a promising author from her new imprint, to read—a story about the Biafran war as told from a child's point of view—while Fidelis rises to give his speech.

His voice echoes in the periphery of Njideka's consciousness as she gets to the part of the book when a soldier discovers the young child in one of the trenches when a hand pulls her up for all to see. The crowd cheers at Njideka like she is a human form of the dollar as she leans on Fidelis' arm.

'Our wife!'

'Beauty.'

Njideka manages a plastic smile as Fidelis begins to explain that they have to be leaving now. She feels her face flush as he puts his arm around her waist and pulls her close, leaning towards the hut's exit.

'What about our son?'

Njideka's plastic smile cracks. She clenches her fists and stiffens her form in Fidelis' arms. Her chest begins to tighten as Fidelis gently leads her to the exit.

'He is on the way,' he says, waving at the crowd as they cheer.

Njideka, trying hard to stop the tears that are threatening to flow, pulls herself from Fidelis' embrace and walks out of the hut as Fidelis follows her.

The crowd cheers even more, like spectators at a gladiator contest.

On getting to the car, Njideka drives off leaving Fidelis stranded.

* * *

Njideka has been pregnant before, once. A year into her marriage, she had gone to the teaching hospital at Enugu because she was feeling sick in the mornings. The doctor did a scan and found not one, but two babies inside. Njideka was happy. She planned to make a room just for the *Ejima*—the twins. She already had name suggestions for them: Osi and Mimi.

Osi is the short form of Osinachi and Mimi is the short form of Miracle. Njideka had always wanted them to have names that were as different as possible because they would share most other things in life, they need not share their identity, too.

Fidelis was the happiest man. When she told him, he carried all 6 feet and 120 pounds of her mid-air while running around their house. He told all his friends to call him Papa Osi na Mimi. He asked Njideka to stop preparing the meals at night and asked their help to sleep over so she could be at

Njideka's beck and call. It reminded Njideka about how hopeful they were as a young couple. When he had promised to give her many children—that she would never regret marrying him.

He had kept to his word on the latter, but not the former, and Njideka believes it's her fault. They lost Osi and Mimi barely two days after she confirmed the pregnancy.

'It's normal for women to have miscarriages during their first pregnancies,' the doctor said. Njideka lay on the table as he scanned her empty womb for any 'retained products of contraception'.

Retained products, he'd called Osi and Mimi, her babies, her seeds.

Seeds that had fallen on the infertile soil that is her body. So, like poorly performing plants, whatever was left of her children was removed by the doctor to prevent her from getting rotten from the inside.

After that, things got harder. They had tried in vitro fertilisation (IVF) several times, took as many traditional herbs as recommended by Nneoma and Fidelis' family members, but Njideka remained without a child.

* * *

Njideka sits in the car and waits. Her clammy palms grip the steering wheel. Her headlights glisten against the shimmering waters of the Osimiri river. The clay and tufts of grass surround the river as it twists and turns, terminating in the bad bush, the evil forest.

There is a wooden bridge, built by the townspeople long ago to aid crossing because it is said that people cannot step foot into Osimiri river without the permission of her priestess. Njideka has been waiting like this for a fortnight. The end of each day brings about the same outcome, only for her to return the next day and wait again, hoping to see Osimiri's priestess.

The first time her mother had told her about Osimiri's priestess, Njideka was but 10 years old. She and Nneoma were sitting around the bonfire under the moonlit sky among thatched huts and dragonflies when her mother told the story of Osimiri.

'Osimiri is our river goddess. She was human, once, before she was turned into water by Chukwu Okike's wife, Uda, as a punishment for sleeping with her husband. She has the power to grant children but only at a price—no one knows Osimiri's price,' her mother said, sending chills down Njideka's young bones.

Nneoma had squeezed her hand and smiled—her calm seeped into Njideka's spine and chased away uneasiness.

'No-one knows where to find the priestess, but it is said she can be seen wherever the river flows and she is drawn to the desperation of those who dare seek her.' Her mother, immersed in her tale, squealed with delight, unsettling Njideka even more, as the story lingered in the atmosphere.

Njideka has never thought of herself as desperate. But she knows that she can no longer bear children on her own. The thought of it makes her clutch the steering wheel as she tries to suppress the bile that mounts in her chest, she looks up at the rear-view mirror and sees the tears that stain her eyes but, instead of wiping them away, she lets them flow.

After the last IVF, she had developed a tummy ache. Fidelis took her to the hospital where the doctors said she had developed a rare complication from the IVF, therefore, they could not risk doing the procedure again. Fidelis decided to stop searching for children then, stating that he would 'rather have her alive than dead over searching for the fruit of the womb'.

Njideka is not one to give up so easily: not when she is so close. Not when Fidelis' family keeps asking for a child. Not when she knows that it is only a matter of time before all her eggs are gone forever.

From the corner of her eye, on the bridge, she sees a plump elderly woman, with snow-white hair and dark skin, clad in white cloth, walking barefoot with a staff in her hand.

Njideka's heart flutters as she alights from the car. The woman's eyes are a ghastly white, and her lips are an unhealthy maroon, like the colour of a bad sore. As the woman walks, she uses the staff to guide her footing, but she still almost veers off the edge of the bridge.

'Nne, why are you alone out here?' Njideka asks. 'You may fall into the river if you are not careful.'

Laughter.

The woman's voice sounds like that of a little child, cackling carried by the winds. It reminds Njideka of her own mother's voice, one that she has not heard in years. Njideka can feel her legs begin to protest, she feels a sudden urge to return to her car and drive home to Fidelis.

'I should be asking you that question,' the woman says as she veers too close to the edge of the bridge again, and Njideka guides her back. Her skin feels cool, like cold dead fish, and the grittiness reminds Njideka of fish scales. The old woman smells like roasted stockfish.

'Where is your house? I can… I can drive you home,' Njideka says, her voice trembling. Her mind screams at her, *Do not drive this witch anywhere! Is this how you crave death?*

'You know who I am, yet you wish to help me,' the woman says, her voice texture changing again, sounding similar to Nneoma's deep throaty voice.

Njideka pauses. She begins to turn when she hears the sound of a crying child. She feels something move in her core as she looks to see the woman placing a hand on her belly.

'My house is across the bridge,' she says.

Njideka looks across the bridge to see a hut that, she could almost swear, appeared from thin air. The hut stands in front of a dying guava tree laced with a few cowries. Njideka guides the woman to the hut's entrance. Each step is excruciating as the sound of the child's cries grows louder and louder in Njideka's mind. Njideka leads the woman to the bench outside and she sits.

'Thank you for helping me, my child,' the old woman says, leaning on her staff. The air becomes still as her face darkens and her lips curl in a grin.

'I know what you want, but I advise you to turn back now before it is too late.'

Njideka considers her smile and feels the familiar uneasiness crawling onto her back and sitting there. Her mind is silent now as if coming to terms with her insanity. She can feel the guava tree staring at her back, taunting her, jeering at her, laughing at the futility of her actions.

Njideka thinks about Osimiri's price. She wonders what it will be, but is already resigned to her fate. 'I am thirty-five. I have had three miscarriages and three failed IVFs. My eggs are almost gone. I have no other way of getting the child I need!'

Njideka catches herself, as her scream echoes across the Osimiri river.

'An impatient person meets his end, yet the wise die in their sleep,' the woman's voice sounds like Fidelis when they are making love—husky, alluring.

'What is Osimiri's price?' Njideka dares.

Her desperation seeps into the priestess' bones. The woman cranks her neck as Njideka's anguished energy moves and lodges there. The priestess licks her lips and swallows, *Oh the glorious anguish!*

'Follow the river to the forest at night when the moon is full and red.'

'Thank you,' Njideka says, stifling her surprise.

'Do not thank me yet. Iji Osimiri ugwo,' the woman says as she blows white dust into Njideka's face.

* * *

Njideka wakes up on the wet soil next to the river. She dusts off the dirt. Her memory dims and turns white as she remembers the dust entering her eyes. She shakes her head and walks to the riverbank to wash her face. The red moon is still against the waters and the river flows, white as milk. She rubs her right hand against her eyes, sure she hallucinates, but the river colour is still the same.

I must be dreaming, she thinks.

Follow, follow, follow.

She hears the voice of the priestess across the river. Then feels it under her skin, a tickling in her nails. Njideka sways past the river to the forest, the nudge to plead with Osimiri is not hers to control.

She sees the priestess at the forest beside her hut, her eyes glowing, symbols forming over her tattooed chest, her skin morphing, twisting, turning. The winds billow against the cowries that hang on the guava tree and one of them falls to the ground and cracks.

The priestess blows into Njideka's face.

White dust. Wakes up.

Njideka follows the river to the forest to plead with Osimiri.

White dust. Wakes up.

Njideka runs. The rivers roars, the moon grows closer, gravity suspended, the forest fertile. Njideka feels time slipping. White dust snows down on her, on the river.

I have to find her. I have to find her. My baby. My baby. Please, Osimiri.

She searches for the old woman's hut, but it has vanished. She calls out, but the priestess does not appear. As Njideka stands in the Osimiri river, the bloodstained crescent moon casts its glow on her face. Her eyes glow white, the river turns blood-thick.

The forest is *in* her, the priestess is in her, Osimiri is in her.

She begins to make her way back home to the river of Fidelis' sperm.

* * *

Waking up in her room, she reaches across an empty bed feeling for Fidelis when an overwhelming ache takes hold of her. She stands in nothing but her panties and ambles toward the exit. Fidelis, dressed in a suit and holding a briefcase, barges into the room.

'Obi'm,' she says, her voice does not belong to her. It is different with a higher pitch than hers, but she does not control the words that follow.

'Where are you going?'

She hugs him from behind, caressing his shoulders and biceps, her warmth seeping through his thick suit. He turns around and kisses her forehead. 'I have a work emergency. They found out I am in Awka and said I should monitor some supplies coming into our port here.'

Njideka strokes his arms.

The sparks of electricity overcome Fidelis' limbs.

'Last night was crazy, Obi'm,' he says, 'Like you were a whole other person.'

Njideka remembers the softness of his kisses, their bodies moving together in rhythm. As Fidelis took off the white cloth she wore to the river from underneath her, she sapped him of his river. She sees the white cloth on the floor in the corner of the room.

Fidelis turns to leave, and she grabs him by the waist and kisses his neck.

'Obi'm, work,' he says, his breath quickening. He turns to kiss her forehead. The kiss trickles down her spine. He kisses her lips and says, 'I love you.'

He turns to leave again, but Njideka feels a new surge of power. She grabs his shoulders, and in a voice that almost does not belong to her, she says, 'Fidelis, I want to have a baby so bad.'

Fidelis lowers his guard, leans into her as he whispers, 'But we are happy together, aren't we? This baby business is doing way more harm than good. You are enough for me, Obi'm.'

Something snaps inside Njideka. Maybe it is all the years of trying and failing—the bruising of her ego and esteem. The fact that Fidelis has never taken the matter of her barrenness as seriously as she has. Or this tenuous tug she feels.

She pushes him away and says, 'This is not enough for me,' and begins to cry.

* * *

Fidelis holds her close to him and wipes away her tears. He kisses her on the lips. She tastes different, sweeter than honey, an explosion of flavours fills his mouth. Njideka returns the kiss, allowing his flame to engulf her. She moves his hand to her ass cheek, and he lifts and places her on the table.

'I still have like ten minutes,' he mutters.

She unbuttons his shirt while he unbuckles his belt. She turns him over on the table and climbs on top of him, riding him, slowly at first, then faster and faster, each thrust sending sensations coursing through his body.

Fidelis enjoys it for a while until he does not. He begins to feel weak, then feels something sucking the blood from his phallus. He looks at Njideka and sees that she has swallowed his phallus. He begins to struggle under Njideka, but it's as if she's growing on him—he feels her weight crushing him.

'Obi'm, stop, it hurts,' he says, as he struggles to pull her off him, but she sticks to him like glue. Her eyes glow a ghastly white.

She moans as Fidelis shrinks under her and she becomes larger.

'Worship me...' she says, only this time it is not Njideka speaking. She continues, paying no heed to his complaints.

Fidelis can feel his life force slipping into her body. He can taste the blood drain from his lips. He tries to wrestle her off again, but she's too strong. She pins him down and keeps fucking him like a possessed whore.

He begins to scream, but she does not yield. He claws at her, but her skin is hard as scales. Her eyes look at him, no longer the eyes of his Njideka, but of something else, someone else.

'Worship me! Worship me!' she howls, her screams and his echo in a twisted melody.

* * *

As she climaxes, his eyes become dark and devoid of life. A faint smoke escapes his mouth, and she inhales it. It smells like life and warmth all bubbling together in Njideka's brain.

She climbs off Fidelis' cold, lifeless body and walks straight into the restroom as if controlled. She catches a glimpse of her reflection in the mirror, as she passes by, with a pregnancy bump, unconcerned. While in the shower, blood mixed with fluid trickles down her thighs. Eyes still white, she washes it all away as her body returns to its normal size.

Njideka hears crying. She grabs a towel from the bathroom stall and wraps it around her body as she runs out, her eyes no longer aglow. The door of the room is ajar, as the stillness offers up a raffia basket on the floor beside Fidelis' limp body.

She treads, a feeling of dread looming at the base of her neck, one foot following the other, until she reaches Fidelis. She falls to the floor, smacks him across his cheek, shakes him frantically. She calls his name: 'Fidelis!'

He does not respond.

She sees the fear in his eyes even in death, and begins to wail.

The crying intensifies, almost rivalling hers, as tiny arms and legs dance inside the raffia basket. Njideka moves closer to the basket. With tears in her eyes, she sees a baby. Its dark skin is wet, covered in amniotic fluid. Its skin feels gritty, like the body of a fish. It lacks an umbilical stump. On its forehead are words written in blood: 'Ugwo Osmiri.'

Missy Hood Tweets

Phil Nicholls

GrannyHood
@MamaHood So sorry, dear, but I feel awful. Taken to my bed. Please send bread and wine.

MamaHood
@MissyHood Gran is unwell! I need you to take her a basket of food. Just packing it now!!!

MissyHood
@MamaHood But Mummmmmmmmmmmmmmmmm I was gonna face time @KitchenElla

MamaHood
@MissyHood You can face your friends later! Basket is packed & Gran is unwell!!

MissyHood
@KitchenElla Going out with basket for Gran so chatz later

KitchenElla
@MissyHood Poor Red chorz neva end
Laterz

MrWolf
@WolfClan WHO OUT HUNTING? WHERE THEM DEER AT? #AnyoneForVenison

WolfClan
@MrWolf Sorry Mate, running the hills today. Good luck in the Forest :-)

MissyHood
@KitchenElla OMG the forest is just so
duullllllllllllllllllllllllllllllll
dull dull DULL
and green

KitchenElla
@MissyHood Clash with the cloak much?
Hope you wearin walkin boots! #NoPlaceForSlippers

MrWolf
@ForestKing WHERE YOU HIDING BOY? GONNA SNIFF YOU OUT! #AnyoneForVenison

ForestKing
@MrWolf I think not, Sir. You crash through the undergrowth almost as loudly as that stompy little girl in the scarlet cloak.

MrWolf
@ForestKing LITTLE GIRL YOU SAY?
#SomethingSmellsGood

GrannyHood
@MissyHood Are you on your way dear? My head is feeling much worse. I am taking a nap. Please hurry.

MissyHood
@GrannyHood On my way Gran but the basket is heavyyyyyyyyy

MrWolf
@MissyHood COULD I CARRY THE BASKET FOR YOU LITTLE GIRL? #WhatsInTheBasket

MissyHood
@MrWolf Uh thanx
No

MrWolf
@MissyHood WHAT BRINGS A LITTLE GIRL INTO THE WILD FOREST WITH SUCH A HEAVY BASKET? #SomethingSmellsGood #WhatsInTheBasket

MissyHood
@MrWolf Take a hike weirdo the basket is for poor Gran

MrWolf
@MissyHood GRANNY YOUR SAY? #LittleForestCottage

MissyHood
@KitchenElla OMG now some creepy wolf dude is stalking me

KitchenElla
@MissyHood Sweetie, you do stand out in that scarlet cloak. Just block the fool and move on.

MrWolf
@WolfClan DON'T YOU HATE IT WHEN PEOPLE BLOCK YOU FOR NO REASON? #Don'tMakeMeAngry

WolfClan
@MrWolf Bad luck Mate, sounds like those piggies all over again :-P

MrWolf
@WolfClan YOU KNOW I ALWAYS HAVE A PLAN? #WolfInSheep'sClothing

WolfClan
@MrWolf Mate, we all know that's code for you wearing a dress :-D

GrannyHood
@Hunter159 Is that you dear? Someone's crashing about in the forest.

Hunter159
@GrannyHood Not me, ma'am. I'm felling trees down by the river.

GrannyHood
@Hunter159 Well somebody is at

Hunter159
@GrannyHood Ma'am? Somebody is what?
Are you alright?

GrannyHood
@Hunter159 YES, YES, FINE DEAR, AND YOU?
MY POOR HEAD MADE ME HEAR THINGS, ISN'T THAT ODD? #NothingToWorryAbout

MissyHood
@GrannyHood I can see your cottage!
Somebodys trampled through your flower beds Not me

GrannyHood
@MissyHood DO YOU THINK I DON'T KNOW? WHY DON'T YOU BRING IN THAT HEAVY BASKET?
#SomethingSmellsGood
#WhatsInTheBasket

MissyHood

@GrannyHood My what long tweets you have

GrannyHood
@MissyHood ALL THE BETTER FOR TEXTING YOU WITH. ARE YOU INSIDE YET? #HurryHurry

MissyHood
@GrannyHood My what large hashtags you have

GrannyHood
@MissyHood ALL THE BETTER FOR TEXTING YOU KIDS. DID I LEAVE THE DOOR OPEN? #MyHeadHurts

MissyHood
@KitchenElla OMG now Gran texting all weird

KitchenElla
@MissyHood Told you the old forest be dangerous!
Take care, girl.

MissyHood
@GrannyHood My what loud texts you have
stuck in caps lock much

GrannyHood
@MissyHood ARE YOU HERE YET? WHAT'S WRONG WITH YOU?
CAN YOU EVEN REMEMBER WHERE THE BEDROOM IS?
#WhatsInTheBasket #HurryHurry

MissyHood
@Hunter159 Are you near Gran's place?
Something freaky happening

Hunter159

@MissyHood Nearly there, Red. Wait for me.

GrannyHood
@MissyHood DO YOU THINK I CAN'T HEAR YOU OUTSIDE? WHAT ARE YOU WAITING FOR, LITTLE GIRL? #ComeIntoMyParlour

Hunter159
@MissyHood I see you, Red.
Wait out front, I'll take a look inside.

GrannyHood
@MissyHood OH NOW YOU COME IN? JUST WALK UPPPPPP PPPP P

Hunter159
@MissyHood All safe now, Red. That wolf won't be bothering you again.

MissyHood
@KitchenElla OMG there was a wolf in Gran's bed
He was texting meeeeeee

KitchenElla
@MissyHood Euww!

MrWolf
@WolfClan WHAT A DAY? #DoNotAsk

Zombie Harold Holt Returns to Parliament

Maddison Stoff

'Now, the Magna Carta is completely clear about the right to return to the country via sea, and also that a freeman isn't to be deprived of his standing via *force*. From what we know about his execution by the CIA, and the subsequent cover-up by the Australian government from the testimony Holt's ghost graciously provided, his rights are in accordance with the *Rights of Spirits Act* of 2083,' the black-robed necromancer starts.

'Her rights,' another black-robed necromancer corrects.

'Her rights, yes, of course,' the first one continues, waving him away. 'We should have a legal claim to seize the state. The *Victims of Possession Act* from 2081 should ensure that her identity is still respected even though she's currently inside Elizabeth's body.'

'Because Elizabeth experienced brain death before donating herself for possession, yes?' the other necromancer says.

'The fact she couldn't use her body anymore herself, plus the contract she signed, grants us the right to consider them a single person under Australian law, yes. Assuming my interpretation of the Acts is accurate, of course.'

'Won't there be questions about if she was coerced into signing that?'

'Maybe, but they can't deny Holt her inheritance without breaking the contract too. The fact that Elizabeth was Zara Holt's granddaughter should help us make our case also.'

I groan.

I keep trying but, for some reason, I can't form words in this body quite yet.

The necromancers look at me with a mix of scepticism and disgust. I don't know if they know I can hear them.

'I still think this is a stupid plan,' the second necromancer says. 'When has interacting with the lamestream legal system ever worked for us before?'

It feels as though I'm seeing everything through fog, or like I'm still under the water. Nothing about where I am or who I am makes any sense to me.

'I spent *hours* in VR researching this,' the first necromancer snaps. 'You think I'll make the same mistakes the sovcits who tried to get that MP arrested for treason did?'

'Which MP? There were a few of them,' the second necromancer says, doubtfully.

'It doesn't matter, Chad,' says the first one, in a mocking tone. 'The point is that my argument is bulletproof… in a legal sense… I think.'

'Zara…' I finally manage to say, remembering my wife.

The necromancers mentioned it was 2092 when they woke me up so this Zara can't be the same one that I married, but it's nice to hear her name remembered, either way.

The first necromancer smiles. 'See? I told you she'd communicate eventually,' she says. 'Zombies aren't unconscious if you put a ghost inside of them, duh!'

Chad shakes his head. 'I think we're both going to hell for this, Marisa,' he says.

'It's better than your fucking idea for a sit-in on their lawn with a skeleton army,' Marisa replies.

'No, it isn't, skeletons are cool!' the second necromancer says.

'It would have got us atomised,' Marisa says. She rolls her eyes and walks over to me. 'Hey, Harold, how are you going?'

I groan.

'Do you think that she's in pain?' Chad says.

'Shouldn't be,' Marisa says, then pulls a strange device out of her pocket and waves it in the air in front of me. 'Her vitals all look fine on my scanner.'

'Do we want to name her something different?' Chad says. 'I'm not sure if Harold or Elizabeth fit?'

Marisa thinks for a moment, then looks at me. 'How do you feel about Harriet?' she says.

I frown.

'We could call you Harry for short,' she continues.

I moan.

'Harriet it is!' Marisa says.

I moan again.

'I think she's going to be popular. I can feel it in my bones,' Marisa says.

Chad makes a disgusted noise.

'Whatever,' he says. 'I'm gonna go and make us lunch.'

'If it works, you're going to be sorry!' Marisa says.

Chad just shakes his head and walks away. I notice, as he leaves, that the Australian Red Ensign flag is printed on the back of his robe. It reminds me of the sea.

I shudder.

'Just us girls then,' says Marisa. She leans in and studies my eyes. 'How are you feeling?'

I moan.

'Don't give me that—we both know you can talk.'

I close my eyes and try to form my words as carefully as possible. 'I… feel…'

'Yes?'

'… tired…'

'Uh-huh.'

'… confused...'

'Yes, yes.'

'… and sad…'

I open up my eyes again. 'Very sad.'

'Do you remember much about your life? Or what you said to us during the séance?' Marisa asks with what I'm choosing to interpret as kindness in her eyes.

I shake my head and look at her, slowly and with difficulty. I'm not sure I even *want* to talk about it. Not with her. But I'm not sure how I'll process any of it if I keep it to myself, and god knows what the world looks like outside…

I find words. 'I remember my old life before I died,' I say. 'But it feels as though it happened to somebody else, and I don't remember talking to you on the boat at all…'

'That's natural,' Marisa says. She nods in a way that comforts me. 'People who agree to merge their consciousness with androids or ghosts often report similar experiences.'

'So there's other people like me?'

'There are people who have merged with ghosts, but not androids,' Marisa says. 'That process was never legal here.'

'Oh,' I say.

'Yeah, the anti-android sentiment is high in Australia, for a variety of reasons. Fortunately, people hate the government that exiled them a little more. We're hoping that will work out in our favour.'

I look at Marisa. She has heterochromatic eyes, hazel and blue, with red hair cut into blunt bangs. She has freckles, and more metal on her face then anyone I've ever seen before. I guess women didn't stop at ear piercing, or got really into it somewhere along the way? I don't understand it and it troubles me. I wish they'd stuck to pastel-coloured dresses instead.

'What are androids?' I reply.

'Fuck, you're old,' Marisa says. 'Honestly, I can't even believe this worked. You're like a living piece of history.' She touches my face. 'Elizabeth was so beautiful too.'

Her touch makes me go cold. Is this woman… *interested* in me? What does that mean?

Marisa pulls her hand away. 'Sorry, that was inappropriate. Elizabeth and I…'

She trails off.

'Well, I guess it doesn't matter anymore.'

Marisa frowns and looks away, then looks back up at me. 'Are you hungry?' she begins. 'I don't know much about what people ate back in your time, but Chad makes an amazing mealworm-cricket burger, if you're interested?'

'No, thank you. I'll pass,' I say, trying to keep my face as neutral as possible to hide my disgust.

'Suit yourself,' Marisa says. 'But I wouldn't turn down free food when it's offered to me, just personally.'

'Is food hard to come by in Australia today?' I ask.

Marisa laughs and shakes her head.

'That's what happens when you let the rich get everything they want and don't make them give anything back in return,' she says. 'There isn't much of anything left anymore.'

'But I *did* support collecting taxes, and I spent them for the betterment of everyone,' I say.

'You were a Keynesian. That's great to compared to heaps of other leaders we had over the next century.'

'But it didn't matter in the end?' I say.

'Of course not,' Marisa says, then laughs sharply again. 'You weren't solving the right problem! But we'll get you up to speed on history after we eat.'

I smell the scent of oregano, cumin, paprika, and vegetable stock in the air. It makes my stomach grumble loudly.

'Are you sure you don't want any of the burgers?' Marisa asks, dragging out the *r* in sure as long as possible. 'They're pretty good…'

I shake my head and sigh. 'Sure.' It doesn't sound like I have any better options.

'Great!' Marisa says, grinning. 'I'll see how Chad is doing and I'll get you one. Don't go anywhere.'

She walks away.

I look around the restaurant that the sovereign citizen necromancers have been squatting in. The windows are covered with heavy metal shutters that look thick enough to shrug off an explosion. The room is lit with cool, white lights and has a lot of strange equipment in it that I've never seen before. I cross my arms and press my body awkwardly against the bar, suddenly feeling very small.

'Here you go,' Marisa says, returning from the kitchen out the back.

She puts a burger down on the counter in front of me.

'You can sit on the stools,' she says. 'They're not going to attack you.'

'But you told me not to go anywhere,' I say, sitting down.

Marisa sighs and marches back into the kitchen.

I look down at the mealworm-cricket burger. The colours look all wrong, but otherwise it's relatively normal, with a brown bun, New Zealand spinach, and a creamy-looking, orange-coloured patty. I remove the upper layer from the bun and look at it suspiciously. My stomach grumbles loudly again.

Marisa resurfaces from the kitchen with a burger of her own.

'You don't have to pick at it like that, you know. It's perfectly safe,' she says, sitting down on the stool beside me. 'We make the buns from native yams and kangaroo grass, and we breed the bugs in the apartments upstairs.'

I close my eyes and bite into the burger. It's eggy, crunchy, and meaty, before hitting me in the face with a bouquet of complex herbs and spices. I've never tasted anything like it before.

'Chad and I used to run the restaurant here, before the war made it impossible to serve customers safely.'

'There's a war on too?' I say.

'Yeah, with America!' Marisa says, through a mouthful of bugs. She swallows it. 'We fought off a land invasion a couple of years back. It's just been drones and missiles ever since.'

'Why are we at war with America?'

Marisa laughs again. 'Let's save the history for later,' she says, as Chad finally comes out with his burger too. He sits beside us.

Chad is dark-skinned, slightly taller than Marisa, and has less metal on his face. But he also wears these wooden earrings that stretch his ears out in a way that I personally find distasteful, and has an intricate tattoo that stops around the top of his neck.

Obviously, men's fashion has changed as much as women's has since the time I was alive, to everybody's detriment. But I never cared as much about what men wore anyway. It's more important who they are and what they do.

'These burgers are surprisingly delicious, Chad,' I say.

'Aw, thanks Li,' he stops himself and swallows, realising what he said. 'Harriet.' He clears his throat. 'Excuse me.'

Marisa frowns.

'So, were you two a couple?' I ask Chad. 'Or…'

Chad looks disgusted. 'No, Elizabeth is my sister-in-law,' he says. 'Marisa and her…'

Marisa punches him in the arm, hard. He stops talking.

'Ow,' Chad says. 'Quit it.'

'You quit it,' says Marisa, looking irritated and uncomfortable.

'Marisa and Elizabeth were *what?*' I say.

A *couple?*

'I don't want to talk about that,' Marisa says. 'She's not around anymore anyway.'

I frown.

'Marisa came to help me run the restaurant after Elizabeth… got sick,' Chad says. 'Marisa's my best friend from way back. We've always all been close.'

'How did Elizabeth get sick?' I ask.

Marisa gets up and slams her hands down on the bar. The plates rattle. 'It doesn't matter,' she says. 'The point is, we want to *do something* about it. You're our chance!'

She takes several deep breaths and sits back down.

Chad puts his arm around her shoulders. 'Are you okay?'

'Yeah, I'm fine,' Marisa says. 'Sorry.'

Chad nods. 'Elizabeth was always sick,' he says quietly. 'It turned into something worse as the supply chains started going down. She couldn't look after herself anymore.'

'What happened to her husband?' I ask.

'Died in the war,' Marisa says. 'Chad told him not to go, but…'

'The man was incorrigible,' Chad says. He shakes his head. 'Still, he helped us kick the commies out of Clarkefield, so I can't say I'm not thankful for his service.'

'Why didn't you go too?' I say.

Chad shrugs. 'Someone had to run the family business,' he replies. 'Anyway, I'm trans, so, the government wasn't exactly knocking down the door to get me out there.'

'Trans?' I feel my heart stop. 'As in, a transsexual?'

Chad raises an eyebrow. Marisa laughs.

'But you don't look like a drag queen,' I say.

'Not that type of trans,' Chad says. 'And trans women aren't usually the same people as drag queens. As for me, I was assigned female at birth. I'm a trans man.'

'Oh…' I say, and swallow my burger. 'Well, good for you then.'

I genuinely don't know what to say to that.

'Well,' Marisa says. 'Now that you know how we are, should we get the history lesson started?'

I nod. 'Ready when you are.'

Marisa turns to Chad. The lights dim, then an image of Australia appears on the rear wall. It has an extra state and looks smaller than I remember it being…

'The history of Australia, by Marisa and Chad!' Marisa says, then strikes a pose.

The presentation is as detailed as it is horrifying, taking me from my death in 1967 to the current year, in 2092. My death occurred two decades before the dominant approach to politics world-wide began to shift away from fact-led, results-driven governance towards two new models for society that focused on reducing how much countries spent on their people, regardless of the impact on their necessary social support services, or the continually-escalating human cost.

These philosophies were known as austerity and neo-liberalism and, together, they led directly to a resurgence of fascism, unmanaged climate change, and the total lack of public trust that authorities in 2092 refer to as the 'death of truth'.

These situations culminated in the world war that Australia is currently experiencing, the complete collapse of our economy, and a biosphere so poisoned by our industry that it's almost impossible to go outside without wearing a climate-controlled suit of one variety or another.

My mouth hangs open while I watch this century of horrors play out on the screen in front of me. Normally I'd doubt it, or interpret it as preachy science fiction, but it actually explains a lot about the way the necromancers who retrieved me from the ocean see the world, and why they look and act the way they do.

The desperation in Marisa's eyes, and the fear in Chad's… That's what happens when the world you live in feels devoid of hope, and you feel as though you've found a way to change it. I don't want to let these people down. I want to help them, if I can.

'I think I understand,' I say. 'You brought me back because I *cared*.'

Marisa nods. 'The nature of your death was also right,' she says. 'Quick and violent. Once we found out how and where it happened, we tracked down your ghost and interviewed it long enough to discover that your conscious mind was surprisingly intact.'

'Not completely intact though?'

'Ghosts don't work like that,' Chad answers me. 'The parts you lacked are still missing, as far as we know, but there are parts of Elizabeth that...' Chad pauses. 'How do you explain modern neuroscience to a zombie from the 1960s?' He sighs.

'You're partially Elizabeth too,' Marisa interjects, sounding annoyed. 'Your consciousness was super-imposed over the parts of her consciousness that she lost due to brain damage. It's possible you're technically a hybrid entity, but we don't know for sure.'

I nod. It sounds insane, but I think I understand.

'She gets it?' Marisa says. 'Really?' She stares at me incredulously.

I shrug. 'I always fancied myself a materialist. How can I help?'

Marisa looks at me suspiciously. 'How long were you listening to us before you spoke?' She gazes at me curiously.

I shrug again. 'I could hear you when I started breathing. I just couldn't use this body right away.'

Chad nods. 'You were out of practice after being incorporeal for so long without anybody messing with you. That makes sense.'

I nod again.

'That's so fucking cool,' Marisa says.

'Hey, I have to ask,' says Chad, looking uncomfortable. 'You're *really* not bothered about being a girl?'

I look down and take in my proportions. 'I don't know,' I say, after a beat. I look up at him again and tilt my head.

'I did my job before I died. I performed my masculinity enthusiastically because that's what everyone expected of me,' I say and then frown again. 'I didn't think I had another option...'

In my heart of hearts, I probably *would* say that I preferred the company of women to the company of men before I died. But every fella would agree they'd rather be a sheila if you asked him, right? That's what Zara always used to say…

Marisa howls with laughter. 'This is going to be *great*,' she says.

'I'm pretty sure that Harold Holt wasn't a trans lesbian,' Chad grumbles.

'How could we know?' Marisa says, her face sparkling with unselfconscious delight. 'He could have been non-binary, easy!'

'What's non-binary?' I ask.

Marisa laughs again. 'Let's get you suited up and march on parliament.'

'The new one or the old one?' asks Chad.

'The old one,' Marisa says. 'They're less likely to attack us there.'

'Are you sure she's ready?'

'She's ready,' Marisa says, standing up.

I groan.

'Don't start that again,' she says, and walks towards the door.

I follow her.

'I've told the other sovereign citizens to meet us at the parliament building,' Chad says, catching up with us. 'They seem excited. And surprised.'

'I told them Spirit Studies wasn't just for cracking into corporate networks,' Marisa replies, shaking her head. 'Did they listen? Nooooo…'

She opens a small compartment on the wall below the stairs to the apartments. It contains a suit on a clothes hanger. She blows off the dust. It looks pretty good.

'I thought you meant we'd have to use those climate-controlled ones you showed me in your presentation?' I say.

'Nah,' Marisa says. 'This is Canberra. The whole city is under one of those weather-control force fields. They don't even get *rain* here unless it's politically convenient!'

I nod. I'd ask for details, but I've learned there isn't any point.

Marissa grins and holds out the suit to me.

'Turn around?' I say. Chad leaves the room.

'I've seen it all before,' says Marisa, before also turning away.

I change into the suit and look at my reflection on the glass door in front of us. My hair is carefully tied back and, despite the cut being a little weird, I like the way it holds my chest and smooths out my physique. I look—

'Presidential,' Marisa says.

I sigh.

'Oh yeah, I should have told you we turned into a republic at some point,' she explains. 'Sorry babe!'

Chad returns from the café holding two pistols. He hands one to Marisa and they hide them in their robes. 'Just in case the government gets violent,' he explains.

'Is the Magna Carta even relevant to your society anymore?' I say.

'As relevant as it's even been.' Marisa shrugs. 'The first step is getting people *interested* again.'

I see her point.

* * *

We walk outside to Constitution Avenue and immediately two silver orbs buzz out from behind some bushes and begin to follow us.

'Press drones,' Marisa explains, totally unphased.

'My post on VR is already going viral,' Chad says.

I don't know what any of it means. I keep on walking. Canberra looks much less overwhelming than the other cities I saw in their presentation.

Actually, it doesn't look too different from how it looked back in my day. There are a few more public monuments, clouds of 3D advertisements hanging in the air, the roads have been replaced with solar panel walkways, and there's more sky traffic than I'm used to.

But the shape of the city, the feel of it, and the way it flows around the underlying land respectfully, in opposition to the violence that created every other city in the country…

All that is preserved here, despite how much the country around it has been changed. At first that makes me happy, then it makes me kinda sad. What's the value of *symbolic harmony* when the country that it represents has been ruined by selfishness? What's the value of preserving somewhere like this, as a promise, when it goes against everything we've ever been and everything we're *going to be* too?

I don't have the answers yet, but, as I walk across the bridge towards the parliament building, I realise that's exactly why I'm here. This world isn't *the future*. That's as far away in 2092 as it was back in 1967, and if anything, I have *more power* to bring this city's promise into action now than anything I could have done from parliament back then.

Nothing I did back then mattered. Nothing I *was* back then matters now. But everything I *was* and everything I am *still counts*, in an abstract way, because it's possible to *use it* while I'm *here*.

We walk down towards Magna Carta Place and even Chad and Marisa look shocked at the sheer amount of people in the park. Swarms of press and advertising drones are buzzing in the air, while giant robots branded with the logo of the Australian Federal Police stalk around the crowd, weapons charged, but not targeting anything.

An organic demonstration starts, led by a person of indeterminate gender with blue skin, pointed ears, a head covered in intricately-patterned scarring, and a megaphone:

'What do we want?'

'Democracy!' the protestors chant.

'When do we want it?'

'Now!'

The crowd parts around us as we walk towards the improvised stage. The protest continues in the background.

'What are we going to tell them?' Chad says.

'I didn't think we'd get this far,' Marisa says, looking worried for the first time since I met her. 'What do you think they need to hear?'

'How about the truth?' I say. They look at me. 'It seems like we should tell them why we're here and then we'll *all decide* what *we think* we should do about it.'

Marisa and Chad smile at each other.

'I *told* you she was ready,' Marisa says.

'I know, I know, I shouldn't have doubted you,' Chad replies, waving at the organiser, who nods and passes us the mic.

The chanting stops, and my new page in history begins.

Cynscout

KC Grifant

She had to find the eggs.

Cynscout blinked alive for the umpteenth time, testing her 4 legs of creaking metal. The pneumatics powered by the fuel cell in her belly warmed her gears, the stretched hide, and bare skull. She glanced behind her to test the iron tail that clanked against the ground.

Satisfied that the body was undamaged, Cynscout trotted out over the hardened volcanic plains of what had once been Vancouver. She shot a message out to the other fifteen Afters across the globe to let them know she was successfully in a new body. The Afters had found that Gold-Retriever-sized military robots—mech mutts—had the best survival rate: 4 legs made them fast, taloned fingers helped them climb, and barbed tails acted as an additional defence. A high-end transmitter built into the mech mutts let the Afters continuously upload backups of themselves if their bodies were destroyed. With the addition of human-like skulls that could create words—should they ever need that archaic communication—the mech mutts provided the bodies the Afters needed to carry out their mission.

And Cynscout was close to finishing that mission.

An impenetrable wall of rock faced her, some new mountain that emerged on the east side of the former city. She calculated the time to climb versus dig, and started to dig.

Next to her, half buried in the volcanic rock, rested the charred figure of a humanoid holding a smaller one, an almost perfect replica of the Pompeii figures she had seen years ago at the Naples National Archaeological Museum. She burrowed a trail under the mountain, the memories of when she was once owner and dog, Cynthia and Scout, flooding back.

Several months ago, she had been a head programmer for one of the largest tech companies on the globe, tapping manicured nails and smiling pleasantly while the CEO screamed in their team meetings. Scout, with his soulful brown eyes and floppy spotted ears, had been the one steady thing in her life ever since she was a teen. The exorbitantly-priced Forever quantum chip she had helped design let her—and other well-off pet owners—infuse clones upon clones of their beloved sidekicks' minds into new bodies.

Never in a million years would Cynthia have guessed that the Forever chip would be her and Scout's pass to surviving Armageddon.

When the strain of a raging contagion and conflux of global superstorms resulted in a brief but effective nuclear war, she and a handful of other quick-thinking pet owners had the same idea. They used the Forever chips to upload copies of their own neuronal patterns alongside of their furred friends and stored their fused personas safely in the remaining satellites. From there, the Afters were able to transmit themselves into various bodies as needed: salvaged computers, industrial robotic arms, and, most recently, the handful of mech mutts remaining across the globe in former army bases.

Now, she and the other Afters carried out the only grim purpose they had come to agree upon: to ease suffering, to help usher in the end of this era. That was the Earth's intent—clearly— and so it was theirs. As soon as they were done, they too would end themselves. The few hundred humans that survived had formed gangs that the Afters hunted, putting a quick end to their brutal fighting for remaining water and carrying out atrocities that Cynscout had erased from her memory in subsequent incarnations. Her heart twisted whenever she thought of the slaughters, but her loyalty to the other Afters and their mission was unwavering.

And the last part of their mission remained: to find the readings of a failed experiment, frozen and now unearthed, that had appeared on their scans. A new signal, self-named 'eggs_genetically_altered' transmitted out an *SOS, help, mayday*. Likely humans, somehow, still trying to survive in a world in which they were not meant to inhabit any longer.

The thought of new life trying to grow and suffering in this burning world made Cynscout stride faster. She was the closest to finding the eggs. Earth had reached the end of its life cycle. So too had everything else. The sooner humans accepted death, the better.

This was a mercy killing.

She loped over what used to be a city block and tapped into a satellite for a global view. The satellites were nearly out of fuel, making their mission even more imperative. All maps ever made of the region clicked through her thoughts from the zettabytes of data they had collected in their shared database. The lab they had identified as being the likely source of the artificial eggs was wiped clean off the globe.

Cynscout moved systematically over the ruins while stretching out a query. **Where are the eggs?** State-of-the-art receptors in the mech mutt let her easily access ripples of information on various wavelengths of whatever might be transmitting. Broken tech with remnants of power tapped out their desperate messages in ever-growing concentric circles—*battery draining, pinging location, looking for owner, searching for network*—all growing closer to silence, closer to the end. She wished them a quick peace.

She stopped when she picked up a sound coming from a pile of boulders. Not boulders—these rocks were pushed together purposefully.

Like a primitive house.

'Stop! Here boy!' A panting solider in an exoskeleton popped out from behind a rock. His voice came through his helmet, hoarse and tinny. Burnt and swollen flesh barely hung onto his face. One arm under his filthy suit was gone, the empty sleeve duct-taped up at the shoulder.

Cynscout felt bad for him. No-one had told him there was no reason left to survive.

'Thank God, a mech mutt.' His voice wavered. 'C'mere so I can reprogram you. Find me some water.'

'This is the end. It's time to go. Your death will be quick,' Cynscout told him. The Afters had found that sometimes a quick explanation helped. Half the time the remaining humans seemed relieved, ready to end it all.

This soldier wasn't. He took a fighting stance and whipped out a gun, sending two blasts toward her. In a nanosecond, she called up tens of thousands of videos, instructional texts, photos, social posts on how soldiers with his model of exoskeleton had been trained. She easily sidestepped his shots and jumped, unsheathing her talons.

She dug her fingers into his throat, taking out the jugular as quickly as possible. His screams of rage gargled to silence. She made a note to delete the look of horror in his eyes—and worse, the emptiness that followed—from her memory the next cycle.

Another mercy killing.

Hopefully, the eggs would be the last. Even though nothing was wrong with her fuel cell, a weariness seemed to settle into her mechanical limbs. She longed to curl up next to the soldier's fallen body and sleep for good.

She peeked into his makeshift stone home in case there were any other survivors. Only a cold stillness greeted her. A singular beep called out, unknown origin. The eggs had started their SOS again.

From right below her.

Cynscout sniffed the dirt and started digging until she hit a door. Steel, melted. She spent the better part of an hour unearthing rubble until she got to the freezer, ten feet below. She wrenched off a thinner sheet of steel and dragged out an insulated bag, tearing it open with the metal fangs embedded in her jaw.

'There you are.' Cynscout spoke the sentence aloud, in case they could hear her. 'This is the end. It's time to go. Your death will be quick.'

There were so many more metallic eggs than she would have guessed. Nearly three dozen—their soft silver puckered like lemons. Cynscout pushed her muzzle closer, taking in as much sensor detail as possible. Human-like, somehow, but different.

She licked one, microscopic pincers on her tongue drilling into the egg, gathering a sample. A mix of human and synthetic stem cells, ready for programming. A quick analysis of a strand of genetic code made her nearly stagger at the information overload. The code had—well, everything.

A gene for an arachnid exoskeleton. Gills for breathing water. Photosynthesis for converting energy. Hollowed-out bones for winged flight. The eggs held all the genetic information humanity had catalogued before its demise. Everything a body might need to adapt, survive.

And, within each egg, a new creature able to execute and manifest traits as needed.

But they were waiting. Half-alive, half-frozen in their perpetual tombs.

The fuel cell in Cynscout's chest glowed as she circled the eggs, contemplating the lives biding their time inside. Posthuman, post-machine. Something more than both, beings that might see vitality in the new world rather than a ravaged one. Creatures that could find it hospitable.

Creatures that could thrive.

For the first time since she had been Cynscout, something flooded her and she didn't turn it off. It was a feeling that made her skull and tongue prickle, her ears tingle, her stomach drop.

'Love,' Cynscout recognised aloud. The emotion activated a chain of sensory memories: their hand/paw playfully swatting Cynthia's giggling nephew; the sun on their skin/fur in the recliner in the backyard; Cynthia's hand petting Scout's ear, dozing together.

Cynscout stood over the eggs, her body warming them.

The other Afters pinged her, relentlessly, *to carry out the mission*. They were coming, they would hunt her if she wouldn't, they warned.

You are malfunctioning, mistaken, misled, the Afters said.

Cynscout hesitated.

She was loyal to them, to their mission. It was a core tenet of Scout and Cynthia threaded together. But there was something bigger now demanding her loyalty. The other Afters couldn't see it yet, even though she could: in Earth's ending she had found a new beginning. And, if they wouldn't see it, well, she would do what she could, for as long as she could.

She switched off comms and funnelled her energy to environmental monitoring while she settled carefully onto the eggs, readying to usher them into this new world when they were ready.

Her mission had changed.

All the Time in The World

Michael Noonan

Professor Joseph Minden acquired his gleaming new limousine at the showroom on West Street. He'd had his eyes on it for some time now. It was expensive and something of a gas guzzler. But seeing that he was approaching his 60th birthday—and feeling in an indulgent and expansive mood—he regarded it as a kind of present to himself. The cheque was signed, and he shook hands with the salesman.

The limo soon had pride of place in his garage.

That night after he purchased the vehicle, he had the most peculiar dream. Not one for generally recalling his dreams—or making much sense of them when he did—that particular one stuck in his mind like a tantalising riddle for which he could glean no answer or coherent explanation.

It began with him walking down a silent stretch of corridor, at the end of which stood a door on which was painted in large, striking lettering: NUMBER 5. He opened the door, expecting to find some room, or chamber, or closet, but instead found himself entering a strange penumbral landscape from which a dark, obscuring mist arose.

He could hear a bell toll in the distance.

He walked through an open gate and found himself in a cemetery, which he recognised was the one where his parents were buried. He made his way through a maze of gravestones and funerary monuments and came at length to a neatly dug grave. A mound of earth stood nearby, with two shovels laid beside it.

Stood by one side of the grave, in mourning black, was his wife, Anna. And stood by her was his son, Clarence, his daughter, Patricia, and his two grandchildren. Nearby stood a clergyman, the book of Common of Prayer opened in his hands.

'In the midst of life, we are in death,' he droned, with a voice as doleful as the peeling bell.

A coffin approached, through the clammy mantle of mist, borne by six pallbearers who proceeded to lower it into the grave, while his wife dabbed the tears from her eyelids.

He approached her and tugged her arm. 'Who are they burying, Anna?'

She turned and glowered at him with neither shock nor surprise. 'You.'

He awoke from the dream, in a sweat, but with a feeling of physical and mental relief at having escaped from it. The strange fabric of the nightmare dogged him all day, until he chided himself for taking such a ridiculous thing seriously. He was a man of science, who believed in reason and rationality above all other things. According to the rigorous principles he lived by, dreams were absurd and senseless things, in which pandemonium reigned and all laws of nature and reason fell to the winds.

Only in a dream, he put it to himself wryly, could a man attend his own funeral, and then still wake up in the morning alive and well. The whole thing was a joke, even if it left a bitter and unpleasant after-taste.

He was a busy man, with other things on his mind. Apart from his work at the University research laboratory, where his expertise in the field of high-tech electronics had been appreciated for over the last 30 years, he conducted, in his free time—in the evenings, weekends, and vacations—his own personal research, in his private laboratory which he had meticulously set up in the cellars of his house.

The walls of the laboratory were soundproofed and the door was always locked, whether he was in or out. And he alone had the key. It was work of a wholly private nature, which he shared with no-one else, discussed with no-one—

and whose results and purposes he alone knew and jealously guarded.

For the past quarter of a century, one subject alone had taxed him in his private research, as an overriding obsession. And that was the question, indeed, the enigma, of time. The complex hi-tech machinery which he had meticulously assembled, activated and tested over the years had no other end but the solution to the challenge he had long ago set himself: namely, to traverse and conquer the element of time—as scientists, engineers and astronauts had managed to conquer the barrier of space, at least within the confines of the solar system.

He was determined and convinced that, one day, he would be able to witness, as if he had been there himself, previous events of history. At the centre of the laboratory was the Screen—the Time-Screen as he called—which would, when fully functioning, be his direct link and conduit to all the past ages of the earth.

He was fortunate to need only 3 hours sleep a night, which gave him plenty of time to work on his project. His work at the University was now only a part-time affair—and the bulk of his energy, and almost the whole of his enthusiasm, went into his private research. He had little or no social life—and few artistic and no political interests beyond his scientific work. His only other real pleasure was motoring. In short, nothing was allowed to hinder his obsession with his private work.

His wife had her own interests and circle of friends. They had agreed, without acrimony or bitterness, to lead separate lives. They only met at mealtimes—and at the odd social occasion—where they had little to say to each other. Indeed, now that the children had grown up and flown the nest, they had little in common with each other.

His wife expressed absolutely no interest in his private research and experimentation in the cellars and she regarded her husband as an eccentric and an oddball, although a quite harmless one, who lived in a strange and impenetrable world of his own.

'If he wants to live like a hermit or a troglodyte, well, that's his business,' she would often tell her friends, if they enquired about her husband.

It was 6 months ago when his tireless experimentation finally began to reach fruition. On the Time-Screen, as he had long hoped and expected, he had picked up images of the past. The forms and shapes were at first clouded and ghostly, as the first television images had been. He could make out little of detail and, at that stage, could hear no sounds through the speakers.

With continued effort and fine-tuning, he managed to sharpen the definition. Slowly, he began to hear the first inarticulate sounds. And then he watched with mesmerised awe as the tapestry of history slowly unfolded before his eyes.

Evening after evening he would tune into the past centuries, as someone else might flick on a channel to watch a favourite show.

In the beginning, the images were only in black and white. But with further refinements and additions to the machinery, colours began to emerge. And the sounds, particularly of speech, became more clear and articulate. But he wasn't content with stopping there. As science and technology had, in his opinion, no recognisable limitations, he had plans for three-dimensional imagery, so that he would be able to see famous figures from the past—whether heroes, villains or saints—as their living contemporaries would have seen them.

He was intoxicated by his own success.

In time, he would disclose his titanic discovery to the public. 'That'll knock Einstein into a cocked hat', he would often growl to himself, with malicious humour. With no-one to share the credit with him, he would patent his singular device, and make a mint in the process, though money had never been his prime objective. His name would go down in history—alongside Galileo, Newton and Darwin—as one of the seminal geniuses of science.

In the meantime, he enjoyed his discovery in private, seeing peoples and societies that no-one had ever seen before. Using a panoply of dials, levers, switches and buttons, he could tune into any era of history that took his interest. He had seen Socrates swallowing hemlock, Plato writing his dialogues, and Aristotle tutoring the young Alexander.

He had seen workers toiling to build the Great Wall of China. He had witnessed famous pharaohs being entombed in their pyramids. He had seen Caesar's legions marching into Gaul, Hannibal crossing the Alps, and the crusaders embarking for the Holy Land.

He had seen Europe laid low by the Black Death. Columbus setting foot in the New World, and Michelangelo painting the Sistine Chapel. He had seen the execution of Charles the First, and the storming of the Bastille. He had seen Napoleon, at the apotheosis of power, crowning himself Emperor, and then witnessed the weary trudge, through the bleak snows of winter, of the Grand Army back from Moscow.

He had witnessed the fall of the Roman Empire, and the sacking of Nineveh. The Titanic collide with the Iceberg, on that fateful night on its maiden voyage, and then sink beneath the ocean waves. He had a ringside seat at the Saint Valentine's Day Massacre and the gunning down of Dillinger.

He had seen the assassination of Lincoln and the murder of the two princes in the Tower of London. Listened to some of the great speeches of history, and noted how little they resembled the enactments of them he'd seen on stage and screen or heard on the radio.

By going back into the past, he had also solved some of the great enigmas of history. He knew the identity of Jack the Ripper, and who it was that assassinated Olaf Palme. He knew where Captain Kidd's treasure was buried, and where King John lost the crown jewels. And he found out why the Mary Celeste was abandoned.

The promethean figures of history, the great scientists, inventers, writers and artists, bloodstained tyrants and dictators, revolutionaries, philanthropists, reformers, and legendary heroes and heroines—Pericles, Scipio Africanus, Cromwell, Leonardo, Dante, Shakespeare, Cervantes, Dickens, Beethoven, J.S. Bach, Florence Nightingale, Lucrecia Borgia, Archimedes, Queen Elizabeth the First, Francis Drake, Blackbeard the pirate, Attila the Hun, Genghis Khan, Hitler, and hosts of others—were as familiar to him as soap stars and media celebrities were to other people.

Yet time, he well knew, had 3 elements to it: the present, in which he lived, the past—which he could now view, at will—and the future, which was yet to come. To witness past ages and events, as he had already done, was a stupendous achievement in itself. But of far greater consequence and significance would be the next logical step in the progress of his invention, namely, to unveil the future, and to bring, to present view, events that were yet to be, and incidents that were yet to happen. But he realised that it would be a far harder task to achieve.

If the future time could be scanned and perused, as he had successfully accessed the past, it could confer the most fantastic benefits on mankind. Humanity would be warned of the perils that lay ahead, or be intrigued and delighted by inventions and discoveries that were yet to happen.

People could be warned about calamities and disasters that lay in store, and of the criminals, maniacs, fanatics and tyrants, whose deadly mischief was yet to occur. Indeed, the Time-Screen could effectively inform man of what alterations he could make to his present lifestyle, and what decisions he could take, in order to avoid future cataclysms—since the future, unlike the past, which was fixed and unchangeable, as history had left it, was the consequence of present action, and could therefore be altered, and improved, in accord with changes in current behaviour.

If he could discern the future, he could save lives and prevent otherwise unavoidable catastrophes from happening. Thus, future time had an entire dimension to it, which past time lacked, for all its historical and educational value.

And on a more mercenary and self-interested level, knowledge of the future could even make him rich. He'd know the numbers that would win the lottery jackpot, and the names of the horses that would win at the racetrack.

It took months of unremitting effort and struggle to meet and surmount that new challenge—but eventually even that barrier was broken—and the Time-Screen was at length programmed to discern the future as easily as it brought to life the past.

The professor's heart pounded against his chest as he activated the Time-Screen, to see the future, for the first time. Though he wasn't by nature a drinking man, he took a bottle of whiskey down to the laboratory that day, and swigged two stiff drinks, in swift succession, to steady his nerves.

Before him on the control-board were the five dials—one for days, one for months, one for years, one for decades, and one for centuries—by means of which he could select whatever period of the future he wished to appear on the screen.

For some unaccountable reason as he activated the screen he remembered his dream, of the night before. He saw, in his mind's eye, the corridor that led to the door with the number 5 painted on it. He saw himself open the door and then step into the strange landscape that lay beyond. He saw himself walk through the same cemetery and witnessed, once again, the mourners beside the grave, and the coffin being lowered into the pit.

He had all the teeming centuries of the future to choose from, and yet, for some reason, he couldn't explain to himself, he turned just the dial for days, to number 5, which would show him the future 5 days from now. Images flickered on the screen and took on greater form and clarity. For the first time in history a man had seen the future, before it happened—even though it was only 5 days hence.

Yet he was aghast at what he saw on the Time-Screen. In his agitation he stood up, cast the chair aside and backed away from the screen, but he couldn't avert his eyes from the images that unfolded.

On the screen was the very cemetery he dreamt of the night before. The bell was tolling in the church tower. His wife, clad in black, and dabbing with her handkerchief her tear-stained cheeks, stood by a grave, next to their son, daughter and two grandchildren. A vicar stood nearby, a prayer book in hand.

'Man that is born of woman, hath but a short time to live,' he intoned.

Six pallbearers carried the coffin and solemnly lowered it into the grave. His wife stooped down, took some earth from the pile by the grave and scattered it over the coffin.

His own funeral, which he had dreamt about the previous night, was now being confirmed by the Time-Screen. In his terror and confusion, a dreadful thought came to his mind. Perhaps the future was indeed as irrevocable and unchangeable as the past. That, just as the past couldn't be changed, so the future couldn't be avoided either. And that we were predestined to live the life that fate had already shaped for us.

His hands shaking and fingers trembling, he switched off the Time-Screen and the ghastly vision disappeared from view. There, on the screen, he had all the centuries before him, but he had only a short time left upon the earth. He felt terror, and indignation.

He shook his head, as a dying man might toss and turn on his deathbed. Had he spent all those long years, day after day, relentlessly building and piecing together that vast and complex Time Machine, only to be shown his own burial, 5 days hence?

He poured himself a stiff drink and drained the glass dry. He felt within himself a raging, all-consuming anger, made even worse by the false excitement and enthusiasm he had felt before activating the Screen. Some things perhaps it was better not to know.

All his hopes and expectations had evaporated away to nothing.

He drank more of the whiskey, until the bottle was emptied. He threw it against the wall, where it shattered into a thousand pieces. He then picked up a hammer and set about the machine, in a wild, drunken rage. All his previous scientist's rationality, had dissolved into the air, and he smashed the screen, the computers, valves and engines.

In minutes he had destroyed a device it had taken him decades of dedicated toil and effort to create. He would be the first and quite possibly the last man to view times other than his own.

He made his way from the cellars up to the surface of the house. There was blood from cuts on his arms and hands as a consequence of his wild bout of Luddism in the laboratory below. He didn't care that he had the house to himself, as Anna was attending a cocktail party at the home of a friend.

He opened the door and staggered out, into the bracing night air. Feeling giddy and unsure on his feet, he lurched over to the garage. He opened the garage door, entered his brand new car, started the engine and drove it out of the garage, down the drive and onto the road.

He wasn't in a fit condition to steer a supermarket trolley, let alone a powerful automobile. But he didn't care. All the pillars and supports of his life had been obliterated by what he had seen on the Time-Screen. And it was as if he was seeking to escape, by means of space and distance, the limitations that time had already imposed on him.

The car swerved from side to side on the road. There were the sounds of car horns and angry voices from motorists and pedestrians alike. But he didn't give a damn.

He put his foot down on the accelerator and overtook a vehicle without checking to see if the road ahead was clear. The car crashed into a large, articulated lorry that was coming the other way. The bodywork of the car was crushed and mangled beneath the weight of the lorry, and it was ploughed off the road onto a nearby verge, where it crashed against a lamppost.

Ambulances and police cars, lights flashing and sirens wailing, rapidly appeared on the scene. The lorry driver was taken to hospital and treated for some minor injuries and lacerations but was soon returned to a clean bill of health.

Witnesses confirmed that the accident was not his fault and so no charges were pending.

For Professor Minden, however, death was almost instantaneous. And the report by the pathologist concluded that the Professor was heavily intoxicated and shouldn't have been in charge of a vehicle.

Minden's wife and family were informed about that tragic incident, and the funeral was arranged to take place in 5 days' time.

His colleagues at the University were astounded at the news of his death, and the bizarre means by which it had come about.

'They say he was steaming drunk while he drove his car,' said Professor Kendal to his colleague, Professor Denton, at the University, the next day.

'And that certainly is out of character,' said Denton.

'I've known him for over thirty years, and in all that time I've never seen him even mildly intoxicated.'

'Yes. I wonder what got into him.'

* * *

One of the police officers, who had called at Minden's house after the fatal accident, and who had then gone down to the cellars and had seen all the smashed-up machinery there, asked Professor Kendal if he would like to see that destroyed laboratory equipment, as it might give a clue to Minden's fatal behaviour that night.

He escorted the professor down to the cellar laboratory. 'I told you it was a bit of a mess, Professor Kendal.'

'You can say that again.'

'Have you any idea what all this stuff is for, Professor? Or why Professor Minden, or anyone else for that matter, should have smashed it all up?'

The professor took his time examining the broken and defunct equipment.

'Well, I don't know why old Minden went on the rampage and smashed all this stuff up. Or why he got tanked up and smashed his car into a lorry. But if you ask me, officer, this is just a pile of junk. Those are the only words to describe it. There's no rhyme or reason to this stuff. And God knows what he was doing down here, with all this paraphernalia. It's like some contraption out of a Heath Robinson cartoon. And it looks like the work of a crank to me.'

He shook his head. 'Yes, I doubt if it added up to much even before he smashed it to pieces.' He looked at the police officer. 'We all thought that Professor Minden was a bit of a weirdo. But he really must have been going off his head. The poor bastard.'

He took a last, lingering look at the dispiriting wreckage.

'It's a great shame. Professor Minden had a first-rate mind, and he could do some really useful work, as I and his other colleagues can attest. What a waste of a great talent.'

And on that sobering note they both left the laboratory and climbed the stairs, back to the surface.

The Portal

Ellen Denton

The portal wasn't a time travel device. It didn't actually send anyone into the past or future, but—by using a person's own engineered DNA—it did provide a means for an elderly person to emerge in the present, at some chosen location, in a young body. More than anything else, it was a toy for the wealthy, who used it to enjoy brief periods of recovered youth.

This is why Mahilia, a 60-year-old technology 'dinosaur', who wouldn't even use hologram machines for intergalactic long-distance calls, first came to use the portal, emerging on a distant world as a 22-year-old girl in a shimmer of beauty before the astonished eyes of her friend.

* * *

She arrived in a white energy field, covered in a viscid liquid that trickled into empty space as cells materialised and swirled into human form.

She momentarily closed her eyes, and when she opened them again, the gelatinous substance sliding down her now fully formed skin had begun to evaporate in sparkly, little wisps. She looked through the energy field into the room beyond, and stepped through it to where Caleb stood waiting.

* * *

'Mahilia?'

'Yes, it's really me.'

Stunned, Caleb approached and reached out his hand to touch her. He gently pressed one finger against her arm as though to test its solidity, and then just stared at her.

She grinned, did a pirouette, curtseyed, and theatrically spread her arms like a ballerina taking a curtain call.

'My God, you're so beautiful! But then, you always were to me, even at your real age. You're beautiful in the only way that matters.' He placed his hand over his heart. 'This is where you will live with me, Mahilia.'

'Oh, for Chrissakes! Caleb, you're a hopeless romantic and you've been watching too many chick flicks. I love you too, but you should be falling to your knees, panting and salivating in dazzled awe at the sight of a youthful me, not spouting greeting card sentiments that were stale before even I was born. Are you even going to offer me a cup of coffee? I'm—'

She never got to finish her sentence.

In one stride he was upon her. They didn't even make it to the bed.

* * *

Two hours later, still on the rug, Mahilia was staring up at the ceiling. She was visibly upset.

'I've never given the portal and its limitations so much as a second thought till now. I couldn't have cared less about all that techno-babble. You know me—I would even joke about 3D hologram machines being "devils work".'

She looked at Caleb. 'Now these things can't be high-tech enough for me. We've only got three hours left.'

There were 3 invariable limitations to the portal. One was that the maximum time a portal traveller could spend in a fabricated body was 5 hours. The second was that they could only do this once every two weeks. Any violations of those parameters would result in severe physical deterioration for the person, first to the temporary young body. They would then snap back into their older body, wherever it was located, which would rapidly experience the same disintegration as the younger one. All the scientific efforts thrown at the problem over the past years yielded nothing to change that.

Caleb propped himself up on his elbow. 'At least we've got uni-mail while you're gone. Hell, we created this relationship using nothing but that for the past two years. What we've built over that time is what's real. This young body you're in right now is a counterfeit coin, not that I'm complaining about it mind you. You'll come back in two weeks, right?'

'Of course.'

'And every two weeks after that?'

'You know I will.'

* * *

The 5-hour time limit was almost up. They stood at the threshold of the reactivated portal.

'I want you to promise me you'll send me a uni-mail the second you get back to Earth, just so I know you made it okay.'

'Yes Caleb.'

'And then a longer one later tonight, like we normally do?'

'Yes.'

'Okay then. Kiss me goodbye, for now. Wait a minute—why do you look sad?'

'I don't—I'm not.'

'Yes, you are. It's in your eyes.'

* * *

Every two weeks, for the next two years, Mahilia stepped through the portal and into Caleb's world for exactly 4 hours and 55 minutes. It always went by too fast, yet in that brief span, on each visit, it seemed a lifetime came and went. They drank each other in like butterflies with only a single season to live, shared their deepest secrets, and made love with unrelenting passion. They sometimes walked in the nearby park and sat in the long, sweet grass of summer, or stood looking at each other with unrestrained love in winter, as snowflakes whispered down between them. If it was night, they would lie back and look up through the skylight of his home at a sparkling galaxy of stars, their hands intertwined.

On one such visit, they made love, and were now at his kitchen table eating dinner. They both started laughing over some funny story he told her, when she suddenly fell silent and looked at him in a way that brought him to a faltering silence too.

'Mahilia, what's the matter?'

She looked away, put down her fork, took a sip of wine and, not seeing any other way to avoid speaking, took a deep breath and looked back over at him.

'Caleb, ever since my first portal visit two years ago, there's something I've known would be inevitable, as far as you and I are concerned, and I've put off talking to you about it all this time, but—well I just can't anymore. The longer we go on, the more this weighs on me.'

'What? What are you talking about?'

'You know how much I love you, right? That will never change Caleb, never. I want you to really understand that, because we're going to end this. This is my last portal visit.'

He sat there for a moment staring at her, until he found his voice.

'You're kidding, right? I know you had that wine, but at 14 percent alcohol, you can't have gotten that drunk.'

He was struggling to make a joke and tried to fake a smile, but couldn't, because something tightened in his chest like an over-tuned violin string.

'Caleb, I know this is something you haven't wanted to look at, but there's a reality we have to face, and I'm sure you must have thought about this too, at least at times. We get to see each other about 10 hours a month,' she said. 'There will never be anything else. We can never have a relationship the way other people do. You can never have a family with me that you can build a life with. You—'

'Wait! Just hold on a second here. Mahilia, of course I've thought about this, and if I gave a damn, I would have said something about it myself. I don't care about a family, and I don't WANT to build a life with someone else.'

'But Caleb, there's no future in this for you. Here, I'm 24, but on Earth, I'm now 62. I've lived a pretty full life. You're 26—your life is still all before you. I need to let you go. I know it sounds like some cliché from a dime-store romance novel, but I love you too much to hold onto you anymore. Dragging out this relationship is only going to hurt more for both of us in the end. The two years I've been coming here to see you have been the happiest in my life. I'd rather keep that as a sacred and inviolate memory, than continue while feeling more and more that I'm monopolising a life that you should be sharing with someone else, or worse, sullying it with the prolonged agony of an impending separation that we both know will come.'

'I don't know that, Mahilia. Even if you died today, I'll still love you. I'm—'

'Caleb, please, don't make this any harder than it already is. You WILL get over me. You will eventually move on.'

* * *

They spent the remaining time they had left of this visit discussing the matter, he adamant in his insistence that they continue the relationship, and she trying to reason with him that, despite the way he might feel about it now, it was for the best that they did n't.

They finally agreed that they would both take a step back and give the matter honest thought, then talk again on her next visit. They held each other and kissed goodbye, then Mahilia stepped back into the portal and returned to earth for another two weeks.

* * *

Every evening, after her return, she took long walks along the nearby riverbank. She always thought more clearly when she was outdoors. It was now the night before her next portal trip, and she still didn't know for sure what to do. She stopped to look up at the sky, her eyes searching for the speck of light she knew was Caleb's home.

Later that evening, she sat down in front of her bedroom mirror. Her long, snow-white hair flowed softly around her face. Time had been gentle to her as she'd aged.

She sat deep in thought, staring into the reflection of her own grey-green eyes in the mirror. Finally, she made her decision.

* * *

After their earlier discussion and her return through the portal, Caleb, likewise, had two weeks to consider the matter. Right after she left, he was too upset to do anything but think about ways to convince her not to end the relationship, if that's what she would again tell him on her next portal visit. But he had promised her that he would step back and give the matter some serious thought, so over the next days, he did. He would take long walks through the park where they often spent time together, weighing everything she'd said and everything he felt.

It was now the night before she would return through the portal to see him. He lay back on his bed, looked up at the stars, and made his decision.

* * *

Mahilia stepped out of the portal and into Caleb's waiting arms. 'Caleb, right or wrong, and hopefully this is more right than wrong, you've got me. At least you do every two weeks for about 5 hours, plus uni-mails. I love you.'

Caleb's face sagged with relief, and then he smiled radiantly. 'Glad to hear it babe, because I had no intention of ever letting you go.'

* * *

The rest of that visit was probably the most meaningful they'd ever had. Caleb felt they'd finally reached a depth of feeling and understanding between them that nothing would ever shake. They made love and then lay facing each other, looking into each other's eyes, shining spirit to spirit, without a need for words. It was a mutuality that many people only get to dream about through all their lonely lives.

* * *

Mahilia stretched her young, portal-generated body gracefully, and asked Caleb if he would bring her some strawberries in a bowl of heavy cream, and make her a cup of tea. She humorously admonished him to be sure to take the time to remove the leaves and stems from the top of the berries, and he humorously responded that 'her majesty's wish was his command', then he left to prepare everything. When he returned, the portal had been reactivated and she was standing by it.

'What are you doing? We still have time left.'

'Caleb, I wanted this trip to be one we would always remember with happiness, not one fraught with five hours of sorrow and farewells. Someday, I know you'll come to fully understand why I'm doing this, and just how much I do love you, and always will. GOODBYE!'

'What do you m—'

He never got to finish the sentence. She stepped through the portal entrance and was gone.

Portal travellers, when the time came to return, simply reversed the procedure and emerged back at where they started in their older bodies. There were 3 invariable limitations to the portal. The third was that it only worked its age-changing magic in one direction.

No young person had ever entered the portal going in the return, opposite direction. This was because tests done with animals on this invariably ended up with the creature—a puppy, a kitten, a baby monkey—emerging and then morphing into a near-to-death, aged, irreversibly damaged body shortly thereafter.

The portal was meant to be a short-term fountain of youth. That's all it would ever be. Caleb knew this well, but he was heartsick at the thought of losing her, and had already made his decision.

He leaped into the portal after her.

* * *

Mahilia almost fainted with shock when she saw Caleb step out of the portal a moment after she did. 'Caleb! What have you done!'

'My God, Mahilia, you are SO beautiful. But then, you always were to me, even at your real age. You're beautiful in the only way that matters.'

He smiled at the memory of her first portal journey to him, and placed his hand over his heart as he had then. Then, he stopped smiling.

'I'd rather have mere days or moments with you here, than a lifetime without you.'

'OH MY GOD! CALEB, NO!'

Mahilia now watched in horror as Caleb began aging with a rapidity so unreal and frightening, it looked like something out of a B-grade horror movie. Every part of him seemed to shrink at once. In the space of under a minute, his shock of thick hair turned white as milk and thinned to limp strands. Wrinkles furrowed their way through his face as though they were live snakes on the run, and his young, straight body seemed to fold in on itself like a collapsing pile of sticks. His internal organs began to deteriorate, until a heart attack sent him stumbling backwards.

Mahilia rushed behind him, caught him under the arms, and dragged him a few feet until, still holding him, she fell backwards into the swirling energy fields of the portal.

* * *

When they emerged back at his house, she could see, even while still enclosed in the energy field, and although he was unconscious, he was back in his 26-year-old body.

She dragged him through and into the room beyond. There was still 10 or so minutes left before her 5-hour time limit would be up. She called for a medical emergency Evac flight-bus. It showed up 4 minutes later and, two minutes after that, lifted off with Caleb in a bio-support chamber.

Torn with concern and sorrow, she stepped back into the portal and returned to Earth.

* * *

Although Caleb had come out of the portal in his younger body, it was too late. The damage to his internal organs was extensive. He never came out of the coma he had fallen into, so was placed on life support in a hospital pod. He was the first and last young person to ever enter the portal going in the reverse direction.

Mahilia, every two weeks, for the next 6 years, came through the portal and spent exactly 4 hours and 55 minutes with him. She would sit by his bed and hold his hand, talk to him as he drifted in unending sleep, or read to him from his favourite books.

On one such visit, it was time to leave, so she got up to kiss him goodbye as she always did before returning to Earth. She was still holding his hand as she leaned over, and suddenly felt his hand squeeze hers. Caleb had woken up.

Over the previous two years, there had been some ground-breaking discoveries in the fields of biology and neurology. Caleb had been one of the test subjects for these miraculous new treatments, and they had slowly but surely regenerated his damaged body.

He eventually made a full recovery.

* * *

For the next 4 years, every two weeks, Mahilia came through the portal and spent 4 hours and 55 minutes with Caleb. They never stopped loving each other, or being grateful for every moment they shared.

Caleb never had any regrets for the time lost that was spent in a coma, or about anything else having to do with Mahilia. He considered it coin well spent. She was the greatest love he would ever know through all his life.

She eventually forgave herself for leaving him that day years before.

More time passed. Her portal body was now 34, but back on Earth, she was 74, and had become riddled with an incurable and rapidly spreading cancer. Mahilia was dying.

She was bedridden most of the time but, as the end drew near, did make one final portal trip to see Caleb, which they both knew would be her last. They didn't make love this time, nor did they speak much. They didn't need to but, instead, spent much of the time clinging together in an embrace, looking into each other's eyes.

Eventually, the 5-hour time limit came and went. The minutes ticked by, one by one. It was night. They now lay side by side looking up through the skylight. He raised his hand and traced the arc of a shooting star for her. She smiled, closed her eyes...

* * *

And opened them back on Earth. Mahilia, her soft white hair spread out against the pillow, looked up through the hospital's glass ceiling at the speck of distant light she knew was Caleb's home, and smiled.

There was a glimmer of happy tears in her eyes, before she closed them one final time.

The FenZone

Ian Whates

I hate them with a passion.

I remember when it was called the Great Fen—an ambitious project to restore a large swathe of land to its 'natural' state, linking together a couple of shrunken remnants of surviving fenland such as Holme and Woodwalton, turning back the clock to recreate the sort of habitat that used to dominate East Anglia before it was all drained for farmland. Those aspirations seem ironic now, given what it actually became.

'Do you fancy going out for lunch?' Tab asked.

'If you like,' I said. 'Where do you have in mind?'

'I thought maybe the Pike and Eel.'

Of course, she did. It was always the Pike and Eel.

'Okay.' I was proud of how steady my voice sounded.

Tab and I didn't connect online, we met in a bar. You know, the old-fashioned way—human to human rather than browser to profile or finger to swipe. This didn't make us unique, but we were a dying breed. I was pants at the whole dating game. I kept getting 'friendzoned'. Every time I built my hopes up, daring to believe that this time I'd made a real connection with someone, the little green heart would appear—never the red one—beating away with its Banner of Doom: 'I like you and I value you, but as a friend.'

I was rich in friends, me, the richest man I knew.

My best mate, Doug, reckoned I was my own worst enemy. 'You're being too honest,' he'd said to me more than once. 'Your avatar looks exactly like you. Your profile always *sounds* like you.'

'That's because I *am* me! What's the point in pretending to be someone else? They'll only be disappointed when they meet me in the flesh.'

'Don't be so naïve. You have to play the game. Nobody's *that* honest. Everybody… exaggerates a bit.'

'Lies, you mean.'

'Exaggerates,' he repeated. 'When you meet someone online, when you bring up their profile, you know that fifty per cent of what's in there is bullshit, embellishments designed to make them seem more attractive, more interesting. That's how it works. When someone comes across a profile as dull as yours and then adjusts downwards for the bullshit factor, what's left sinks way below the level of boring. It's as if you're trying to push romance away, not invite it in to sit down and say hello.'

He didn't get it. 'I don't want to meet someone like that. I can't be the only person in the world who's after a relationship based on honesty rather than…' I was trying not to say 'lies' again.

'Embellishments,' he supplied.

'Exactly.'

'Look, all I'm saying is… jazz it up a bit. Insert a few nuggets here and there that are obviously blowing smoke and not meant to be taken seriously. Make 'em humorous and people will love you for it. That way, you won't be misleading anyone, but you'll still be showing a bit of personality, rather than just parading a list of drab facts guaranteed to get them flicking to the next profile. I can help you with the wording, if you like.'

My lack of enthusiasm must have shown. 'At least promise me you'll think about it.'

'Okay, I will.'

We both knew I wouldn't.

* * *

Our ability to adapt as a species never ceases to amaze me. In defiance of every portent, we wreck the world's climate and move on. In the space of a few years we accommodate the impact of Covid and move on. In the space of a few decades we leap from the pedestrian awkwardness of first generation analogue phones to sixth generation instant connectivity and hardly miss a beat.

We build a wall around a supposed nature reserve after declaring it a deadly no-go area and nothing changes, even for those of us who live in its shadow. Oh, there's been consternation, questions, speculation, a brief outburst of fear and outrage, but, essentially, we shrug our shoulders and get on with our lives. Most of us do, at any rate.

I first met Tab at a bar in St. Ives—not the picturesque Cornish resort that's always in the newsfeeds, tugging at the heartstrings as it wages a losing battle against rising sea levels. No, I live in the market town near Cambridge which is forever associated with Oliver Cromwell. Here there used to be a cluster of pubs and bars where Broadway splits to become Crown Street and Merryland: Floods Tavern, the Lounge, the Royal Oak… all gone now, swept away by the Covid pandemic, victims of humankind's retreat into the digital. But the Nelsons Head still survives, and that's where I ended up on this particular rainy evening, seeking refuge from both sodden skies and the prospect of another night spent home alone with a ready meal.

The bar was practically empty. The only patrons were a couple occupying a table near the fireplace at the back, a young woman perched on one of the plush padded barstools, and me.

I chose to sit at the bar, four empty stools separating me from the woman, and tried not to study her too overtly. She intrigued me. What was she doing here alone? Not waiting for a friend—there had been no glances towards the door since I arrived, not even when I came in—so perhaps she was taking refuge from something, or someone.

A glass of pale golden wine, which I imagined to be Pinot, sat on the bar in front of her, barely touched, and her posture—hunched slightly forward—meant that most of her face was obscured by long dark hair that hung straight down like a veil.

Realising she was never going to glance up long enough to make eye contact, and despairing of her ever finishing that wine, I took the plunge, standing up before courage deserted me to stride over and claim the stool next to hers.

Doug was shocked when I told him about this the following day. 'You did what? *Are you mad*? Going up to a complete stranger like that…?'

I shrugged. 'It felt like the right thing to do.'

She didn't seem phased in the least by this man plonking himself down uninvited beside her and trying to strike up a conversation. Okay, so she didn't seem especially thrilled by my approach, either, but I'll settle for polite any day.

Her name was Tabitha, Tab for short. I can't pretend there were fireworks or that she gave any indication of fancying me, but conversation happened and at the end of the evening we arranged to meet again. Looking back, I suspect that's the whole reason she was there: to connect with someone like me.

That was two years ago. We moved in together 6 months later, or rather Tab moved into my place. She's a couple of years younger than me, and there's a hint of Asian or perhaps eastern European heritage in her features which I've always found attractive, but she told me she was born here in the UK. She doesn't like to talk about her childhood, which I gather wasn't a happy one.

'The weather's looking good today,' she said as I drove us towards the Pike and Eel.

She always said that. We only ever came here when the weather was good.

'We can sit outside, if you like,' I suggested—my pat response.

'That'll be nice,' she said, completing the ritual.

We were happy, in our own fashion. For two years we had pointedly ignored each other's eccentricities and played at being normal, which is ridiculous because I've never been that, and I'm pretty sure Tab was as far away from normal as you could get.

For me it was the sense of being out of sync, a feeling that I had somehow been left behind as the world raced forward into a connected future. It was probably why I felt such an affinity with the Great Fen project and its dogged determination to turn back the clock—Canute standing against the tide.

I've always felt out of step with the rhythms of modern-day living: an analogue spirit in a digital age, a 1G person stranded in 6G reality. Initially, I thought that in Tab I'd stumbled upon a kindred spirit, but the longer we were together the more apparent the differences became. Now I think the opposite was true, that the world had yet to catch up with her. Maybe it was a case of opposites attracting, or maybe I was just convenient.

A traditional country pub, the Pike boasts 6—always 6—wooden tables with attendant benches, arranged haphazardly on a long lawn that runs down to the river. There were two other couples outside when we arrived, one with young kids running around, but Tab was able to claim our 'usual' table while I went in to fetch drinks—a pint for me and a large glass of Pinot for her—I'd been right about that much on our first meeting, at any rate.

I came back to find her staring across the river. At the wall.

'You look lovely today,' I said as I put the glasses down and sat opposite her.

She sat too. Glanced at me, smiled and said, 'Thank you,' before turning her gaze back to the wall.

That was what she always said, whenever I complimented her appearance, her cooking, her anything. Never, 'It's a new top, I'm glad you approve,' or 'I found the recipe online and thought you'd like it,' or even 'You look pretty good yourself.' Just: 'Thank you.'

I studied her face in profile and wondered again who she really was. I'd never been introduced to any of her family: 'We're not close,' and only knew the sketchiest details of her past. She, on the other hand, had heard all about me, had met my mother (my father having passed away years ago), who professed to love Tab. Mind you, I think she would have loved anyone who was willing to put up with me, and Tab had briefly met my sister, who declared herself thrilled that I'd found someone 'as creepy as you are.'

Tab was polite to both, without ever really paying attention to either of them. Those meetings only reinforced my conviction, which had been gathering for a while, that there was something fundamental missing in her.

Many of the things Tab said were spoken by rote—she seemed incapable of making her comments sound spontaneous or in any sense personal; either that or she couldn't be bothered to do so. Sometimes I pictured her as the outer shell of a person-size Babushka doll with all the smaller dolls removed from inside of her. Perfect on the surface but hollow, the deficiency unknowable until you split her open to reveal the dark void that lurked within.

I took a sip of beer and let my gaze slide away from her face to take in the water and the wall that rose beyond it. I didn't doubt this was why she felt so drawn to the Pike and Eel, though we'd never spoken of it—we didn't do confrontation.

For a few silent moments I joined her in contemplating the FenZone, its imposing grey-green wall marching along the far bank of the river. No pub or restaurant stood closer. I resented that place deeply—for the way it had hijacked the Great Fen project and corrupted it into something dark and twisted.

Initially, the project had been a spectacular success, delivering everything that had been promised: endangered beetles and aquatic invertebrates, otters and water voles, bitterns, harriers, short-eared owls, shrikes and bearded tits all colonised the area, as did a variety of ducks and terns, and even a few cranes on the reserve.

Then something else moved in.

Nobody knows what, or at least nobody is admitting if they do know, but its presence was pretty hard to ignore. Equipment started failing—not just a matter of one or two things conking out here and there but on mass. Then people started dying: wardens, visitors, those working to expand the reserve—dozens of them—and they were just the first.

What killed them is shrouded in mystery—a blanket of official secrecy thrown over the whole thing. Police went in. They died. Soldiers went in. They died. Drones were sent in. They crashed. Scientists went in swaddled in hazmat suits, their equipment shielded from EMPs and protected in every way conceivable. The equipment failed. The scientists died.

The authorities tried to hush things up but, in this digital age, that's pretty hard to do. They would have had to crash the whole 6G network to achieve that and, besides, it was too late. No-one had thought to keep the first deaths quiet, so public attention was already focused on the fen.

In the vacuum of official information, it was inevitable that rumour and conspiracy theories would proliferate. The sort of wild speculation that I would have dismissed as hilarious not so long ago suddenly seemed all too plausible: the heavy-duty work to rebuild the habitat had unleashed an ancient virus that had lain dormant, locked inside fen mud since the last ice age (but then why hadn't there been a pandemic like Covid, spreading to claim lives beyond the fen itself?); the authorities had uncovered something so dreadful that they were killing everyone who had seen it (I don't have much faith in politicians but my mistrust hadn't yet stretched that far); the Chinese had created a deadly new weapon which they were trialling in the Great Fen (in my parent's time it had been the Russians, these days it was the Chinese, but their technology already underpinned our lives, so why would they need a clumsy weapon when in all likelihood they could bring our entire 6G world crashing down around our ears with one simple command?). Riffing off a couple of the other theories was the suggestion that an ancient alien weapon of mass destruction had been unearthed. Either it was killing anyone who came into contact with it, or the authorities were doing so to keep its presence a secret (a counter-productive policy if ever I've heard one).

Then there was the theory that something completely 'other' had moved into the fen, that by chance the restoration had provided the ideal habitat for alien visitors newly arrived on Earth—the right place at the right time, sort of thing. Applying Occam's razor, you'd think this one was a non-starter, but once you've discounted everything else… Scoffers asked why these hypothetical travellers hadn't announced themselves, why they hadn't contacted the world's leaders. Perhaps they had, or perhaps they had no interest in doing so—just because that's how we would have acted doesn't mean another race would rationalise in the same way—or maybe they just mistrusted politicians as much as I did.

Of all the crazy theories doing the rounds, this was the one I found hardest to dismiss.

'Shall we go for a walk?' Tab asked once we'd finished lunch—freshly-made sandwiches in crusty white bread. I'd gone for smoked salmon this time around, Tab for her usual cheese and pickle. We'd both left the token salad garnish untouched.

'Why not?' I replied, as I always did.

The walk consisted of us heading down to the river and strolling along the bank, away from the pub. The FenZone wall was even closer here, even more imposing. Metal grates formed filters beneath the wall in places, allowing water from the fen to drain into the river, so whatever was being kept in wasn't reckoned to be that small. Birds could still fly over it, of course, so aerial escape wasn't considered a risk either.

I held Tab's hand. She didn't object. Her grip in response to mine was soft and languid.

The wall hadn't been the only solution considered. There were strident calls for military action—jets, missiles, even a tactical nuke were all proposed. Perhaps some of them were tried—who knows? —but, if so, the technology proved no more robust than that which had gone before, and the munitions failed to detonate. In the end it came down to the wall. If we can't blow the problem up, let's settle for shutting it away so that we can pretend it doesn't exist.

Well, perhaps not entirely: a few miles to the north of the Pike and Eel a 'compound' had been erected, attached to the outside of the wall. High fences, armed guards, grey squat buildings, and vehicles with darkened windows sweeping in and out at all hours. From here, presumably, they continue to study whatever is in the fen, or try to at any rate. I've no idea how they do so or with what degree of success.

They seem convinced that the wall is fit for purpose. I'm not so sure. I mean, at the end of the day it's just a wall, no matter how big and impressive it may be. I also wonder what might have escaped from the fen before the wall was completed or before it was even started.

* * *

Two days before this latest trip to the Pike and Eel, Doug had asked me to pop round, saying: 'I've got something to show you.'

He ushered me into his front room, which was dingy and cluttered at the best of times, but today he had the curtains closed, despite it being a bright afternoon.

'What's with…?' I gestured towards the windows.

'Oh… You'll see,' he assured me. As soon as I sat down, he began. 'You know we're living in a 6G world, right? Do you really understand what that means?'

'Yeah, of course I do.'

'Okay,' he said, evidently unconvinced. 'Think of it this way: the first generation of mobile devices, 1G, used analogue technology—it liberated us from our dependence on the landline but that was about it. Then 2G introduced us to the joys of texting. And 3G gave us access to digital services and broadband, while 4G was the culmination of that particular evolutionary path. It enabled us to do all the things those earlier generations of tech could do but faster, better, and with added bells and whistles.'

He looked at me.

'Fifth generation is where we really started to kick ass. But 5G wasn't just an upgrade on what had gone before, it was a giant leap forward, a whole new concept. It took away our reliance on those old cell phone masts to get a signal, because aerials are now everywhere—on the corners of buildings, traffic lights, lamp posts—and they communicate with each other and with us all the time. Billions of new devices came into play with the launch of 5G.'

'And 6G?' I prompted.

'An upgrade which became necessary when 5G didn't quite deliver the seamless flow of information that had been promised, while the ability to regulate human activity—to smooth things out for the benefit of us all—proved a lot trickier to action than it had been to plan. But 6G has taken care of that, with its saturation of even more aerials and the introduction of newer, slicker software.'

I didn't have an answer for him.

He wasn't waiting for one. 'Your car avoids potential accidents by governing the speed you drive at, taking into account the road conditions for miles around, and it will steer away from a cyclist if you haven't seen them, while your fridge orders standard groceries when you're running low without even consulting you, and your health is constantly monitored—blood pressure, stress, sugar levels… We're used to these things, to an integrated way of living, but have you ever stopped to consider the wider implications? All this info being constantly generated and shared, an inconceivable volume of it, means that the system knows where everybody is, all the time. Everybody.'

I had been aware of this, or most of it, at some level, but to have it spelled out so starkly was chilling.

'Look, let me show you.' He summoned up a real-time image of the two of us, sitting there in his room. 'There's you and me.' He waved, to prove the point, the image mirroring the gesture. 'Now watch.' Two long strings of digits and symbols appeared, superimposed on the image, to scroll rapidly across our view. 'That's how the system sees us, you and me,' he explained, 'our personalised coding, unique to every individual. Now watch this.'

The image of Doug and I vanished, to be replaced by a view of a car, my car.

'This is from last Tuesday.' The image adjusted constantly, handed over from one receptor to another as the car moved down the street. You could clearly see me driving and Tab beside me in the passenger seat. 'Recognise it?'

'Sure, of course I do.'

'Okay, and what do you make of this?' As before, a string of code scrolled across the screen. Just one string. 'That's the system recognising you—the same unique coding.'

I didn't want to say the words, but eventually they crept out. 'And Tab?'

'Nothing. Zilch. Apparently, she doesn't exist... I mean obviously she *does*, we can see her right there,' and he gestured at the image, 'but she's a black spot as far as the system's concerned. It doesn't recognise her, doesn't even acknowledge her existence, and that's impossible.'

'Then how...?' I looked at him, desperate for an explanation.

He shook his head. 'I have no fucking idea.'

* * *

As with so much else involving Tab, our post-pub walks always followed the same routine. We would stroll along the bank for the best part of a mile, avoiding all mention of the imposing barrier just a river's-width away, while commenting on the ducks and swans that we passed, the cormorant with its great black wings outstretched to dry in the sun, the moorhen that weaved in and out of the reeds at the margins of the water, trying to chaperone its unruly brood of chicks.

Then we'd climb over a stile and follow the footpath that led away from the river, with fields to our right and woodland on the left, before cutting through the woods and back to the Pike and Eel and its car park.

This time I wanted to shake things up a little, to see how she'd react. As we stepped away from direct sunlight and into the shade of the trees, I stopped walking and placed a hand on her shoulder so that Tab stopped too. The world fell silent. No-one else was about.

She looked at me, surprised, curious.

'You really are beautiful,' I said.

'Thank you.'

Her full lips beckoned. I leaned forward and kissed her. She accepted without really participating. I broke the kiss and rocked my head back a fraction so that I could look at her. A half smile formed at the corners of her mouth, and the curiosity in her eyes remained.

I got the impression that Tab was intrigued by this break from our customary pattern.

My hands rested on her hips. I moved them up, slowly, feeling the slenderness of her waist, the swell of her breasts, marvelling at how solid, how real, how perfect she felt. We kissed again. This time she seemed more responsive, but perhaps I imagined that. When we broke for air, my hands were on her shoulders. Her eyes now seemed to shine.

I moved with deliberate slowness, bringing my hold closer together until my fingers circled her throat. I paused, staring at her, and then began to squeeze.

She didn't resist, didn't squirm or struggle, didn't bring her own hands up to try and stop me. She didn't cry out, 'Stop!' or 'What are you doing?'

She just stood there, her gaze locked onto mine.

I have my own theory about what has seized control of the FenZone. I don't think they're intrinsically hostile to human life, I just think they've staked a claim and are consolidating their territory. They're making sure nobody challenges their right to be here, to possess the fen. Small creeping things and birds on the wing aren't a threat, but humans, with our machines, with our determination to manage and constantly manipulate the environment, we are. So they cleared us out, stymied our technology and removed our ability to interfere. Nothing malicious, just being practical.

The thing is, I've a feeling that's not all they did. Yes, they'll leave us alone so long as we don't trespass, but if this is to be their new home, wouldn't they want to learn a bit more about the neighbours? Quietly, without causing a fuss or raising the alarm.

It seems to me the best way to do that would be to live among us, to study us up close and personal.

Stands to reason that they wouldn't get the mimicry right in every regard, not to begin with, but given that they possess the technology to cross between stars I bet they wouldn't be far off. Not perfect maybe, but close enough to pass for human. Almost.

I'm not sure at what point Tab stopped breathing, but her eyes remained open, staring straight at me, and the light within them never wavered.

Free from Want

Jeff Somers

'What are you going to do?' Hal asked in that bright, mocking way of his. 'Go live off-grid? That's basically suicide.'

She winced. He meant suicide for someone like her, of course—someone who would never be capable of surviving outside the support of civilization. She had no doubt that he believed *he* could live off-grid and be just fine. *He* hadn't spent the last few months in a rehabilitation center, being... *cured* was the wrong word. Adjusted? Re-calibrated? Shamed.

Seeing her expression, he softened. 'Oh, shit—look, kiddo, I'm sorry. But for the time being you simply can't find an apartment without a Fabricator. Look—I'll disconnect it, okay?'

She hesitated, then nodded. She knew he had taken time off to fetch her, to find her a place to live. She had to at least *act* grateful.

'Okay,' she said, summoning as much energy as she could. She watched him walk over to the glossy white rectangle and start examining the casing. She couldn't explain the fear she felt, looking at it. She remembered the mantra from her rehab stint: *All you had to do was nothing.*

She did nothing. It was harder than she expected. Watching Hal struggle to remove the Fabricator's outer wall, to once again impose himself on the situation, she wanted to stop him, to beg him to leave and then begin to work with the unit, to push it, test its limits.

She saw the room full of pink unicorns and shuddered, a mix of fear and excitement sluicing through her.

Closing her eyes, she did nothing.

* * *

Alone in the space, with Hal's cigarette smell hanging in the air, she felt agitated and restless. She moved around the unfurnished place, but kept coming back to the kitchen. Eventually she gave in and settled there, sitting on the floor in the small, all-white room.

At the rehabilitation centre, they'd lectured on the history of the kitchen. She'd seen photos of historic kitchens with their appliances, and knew they once only served as a food storage and preparation space.

She rolled the unfamiliar word around: *Cooking*. To cook. A way of preparing food for consumption.

To cook. Remembering the word made her hungry. She stood up and approached the Fabricator. Her heart pounded. She felt the mixture of desire and repulsion. She licked her lips.

'Cheeseburger, rare,' she said. 'American, brioche, ketchup, lettuce, pickles.' She paused. 'Wine, Cabernet, fruit forward, room.'

She waited for the soft thing, the warm red glow, The Voice repeating and confirming her instructions. But the Fabricator remained silent and dark.

'Oh,' she said, remembering Hal working to disconnect the machine. 'Oh.'

She felt grief, and began to cry.

* * *

Living without a Fabricator was difficult, but not impossible. Food was easiest. Plenty of places claimed copyrighted recipes you couldn't download to home, so eating out was an expensive option.

She struggled with menus. Anything basic and normal was easily retrieved from the Fabricator at home, so the dishes available outside were unique and seemed aggressively strange, as if designed via algorithm by an artificial intelligence that lacked the ability to taste or digest.

Starving, she retreated to the empty, antiseptic apartment. It lacked furniture and other essentials, and every moment brought a new frustration. She stepped out of the shower and thought of towels. She sat on the floor and contemplated a bed. She called Hal but, of course, he was unreachable—her perfect brother out being normal and carefree, happy and whole.

Heart pounding, her mouth filled with the taste of metal, she stepped into the kitchen and began working to put the Fabricator back together. It didn't take long. Hal, conscious of the penalties for property damage (and that the apartment had been rented under his name) had been gentle and unimaginative with his sabotage.

When the Fabricator glowed a warm, dark red, she licked her lips. Excitement filled her. She opened the reservoir in the back of the machine and extracted a sealed foil packet of matter. The Fabricator could use anything, and the most common sources for raw materials were garbage, roadkill, and other unsavoury things people generally didn't want to think about. You could put anything into the reservoir and the Fabricator would re-arrange its atoms into whatever you specified, but most people preferred to think of the blank foil packets as fuel, with no specifics. She slid the packet into the slot, as she'd done thousands of times.

'Cheeseburger, rare, American, brioche, ketchup, lettuce, pickles,' she said. 'Wine, Cabernet, fruit forward, room.' She hesitated. 'And... a Shirley, file number 55682287_Glee.'

The Fabricator glowed green, and she smiled.

* * *

'I'm not running a *program* here,' the fat man complained. 'I just manage the apartments.'

'Okay,' Hal said, keeping his voice as neutral as he could.

'Not my job to monitor when the tenants come and go.'

'Okay,' Hal said again, hoping for some combination of tone and politeness that would result in an escape from the conversation. 'I only meant that it's why I'm bothering you. Because I know it's an inconvenience. I wouldn't do it except I have access to her citizen data, and I can tell she hasn't left in three days. I didn't mean to imply anything.'

The manager sniffed, swinging his master pass card by the lanyard. 'If she's under order to store her Biometrics, buddy, you're legally supposed to inform me.'

Hal shut his eyes and asked the universe for strength. 'I know. I am sorry. I didn't think that she'd be any trouble.'

At her door, the manager swiped his card and the lock clicked open, loudly. But the door remained steadfastly closed.

The manager frowned. 'Huh. Strange.'

He pushed against the door, giving it a real effort. It slowly inched inwards, the gap filling up with bright pink fur.

'Oh, no,' Hal said.

With a grunt, the manager got the door open, and a dozen pink unicorn plush toys spilled out into the hall. A wall of similar toys filled the entryway from floor to ceiling.

The manager staggered back. 'What is this?'

Hal stood, frozen, uncertain. His florid, handsome face was wide open with an expression of fear.

'It's her Shirley,' he said.

* * *

He remembered it. The original. A pink plush toy their father brought home one night just a few weeks before his suicide, handed over to his daughter with a wordless, oddly formal deference. It was not—had not been—fancy or even particularly well-made. It was hard and uncomfortable, the pink fur abrasive and scratchy. The face had always seemed kind of disturbing to Hal, the plastic eyes off-centre and the felt red mouth locked in a grimace.

But Hillary loved it on sight in her little girl way. She named it Shirley and commenced carrying it with her everywhere.

After dad opened a vein and ruined the bathroom, mum insisted on remodelling despite their endless money troubles. Shirley became Hillary's main memory of their father. She always had it, often carried on long, convoluted conversations with it, and screamed if Mum tried to wash it even after it had become threadbare and stained.

In her teen years, she kept Shirley on a shelf above her bed, and took it to college with her. Hal had felt sympathy for all the boys struggling to unhook his sister's bra under the crooked gaze of Shirley the pink unicorn.

* * *

They'd been one of the last families in their neighbourhood to get a Fabricator. The original models were incredibly expensive, and their father left them nothing but debt. A series of smaller, and grubbier homes followed, and if Hal had to admit that their mother pulled herself together and navigated their reduced circumstances as best she could, he also thought she had done so without much grace or good humour.

He was a senior in college when the house acquired a Fabricator, and Hillary was entering sophomore year, carrying Shirley back and forth with her between home and campus. After a few days playing around, making roast chickens and random toys appear, Hal had what he thought was the best idea of his life.

Sneaking Shirley out of his sister's room, he scanned it from every angle, saved the template, and printed a new one, fresh and clean. He felt particularly virtuous about resisting the urge to fix the thing's horrific facial expression.

Hillary was touched and excited. And, to his surprise, she kept *both* Shirleys.

A few months later, the college called concerning the first seventy-five Shirleys Hillary had printed. While the school couldn't detail the specific rules she had violated, it was clear she wouldn't receive a housing assignment without a fight, so she returned home to attend the local Community College.

The problem got worse as Fabricators became more common. Hillary got into the habit of printing a Shirley any time she felt anxious or lonely. When they had to sell the house, Hal remembered throwing more than a hundred Shirleys into a big green dumpster.

* * *

They tunnelled. Working together, they crawled through the stuffed animals, tossing them into the hallway behind them. The manager fought his way to the window and began to hurl the Shirleys into the street below. Hal detected the familiar hum of the Fabricator, and began fighting his way towards it.

The toys were treacherous, sliding away and giving inconsistently. It was like being buried under enormous grains of sand. With effort he clawed his way into the kitchen, found the red-hot appliance, and managed to switch it off.

He sagged back against the wall of plush unicorns, breathing hard. He dragged a hand over his face and felt the sticky wetness and froze. He kept his eyes closed. He could smell it, then, the coppery scent of blood. He squeezed his eyes more tightly closed, because he didn't want to see, but the suffocating press of the toys made him desperate to move, to get up and escape into emptiness, into space.

He saw her, relentlessly making them. He saw her, becoming trapped in her own apartment, the apartment he'd found her, the easy place he could afford for her because finding any sort of shelter without a Fabricator was impossible, or nearly so.

He saw her making the calculations: If she tunnelled out, someone might see. Someone might ask questions, or call him. If she left the apartment, her biometrics would have shown where she went, and then he would have known she was buying matter packets for the machine, and he would have guessed why.

So she'd stayed. And used every possible bit of matter to feed the Fabricator and make the Shirleys. Because Fabricators weren't magic. They needed mass to transform.

Keeping his eyes closed, he started to crawl blindly away. He imagined she had started with her toes.

The Fifth Awakening

Patricia García-Rojo (Translator: Mike Lucas)

The Earth cleans what progress has dirtied.

The mouse has made its nest inside the robot's head, showing among the flowers like a mechanical skull. Every spring it becomes harder to find it in the oak clearing where the moss spreads over the broken wing of the old Hope B15. It will take just one generation for nature to bury the remains of the battle, for the forest to engulf humanity's terrible past. Then everything will be back in its place.

Edelvina Canto nods, satisfied. Then she lets out one of those deep calling whistles and starts walking back to the village.

She always goes to the oak glade before a meeting of the Council. This helps her to remember, to gather herself. For her, that wrecked ship and the fast-disappearing mutilated remains of the robots spread out among the grass are the altar before which she needs to prostrate herself.

But no-one uses the old formulas of the messianic religions anymore. No-one believes in a benign implacable universal entity that observes the world from the outside. Now new words spring from the lips of believers.

'For a green kingdom,' murmurs Edelvina.

A big, lanky cinnamon-coloured dog comes up to her with its tongue hanging out, waiting for a touch from her hand.

'Found something, Olmo?' Edelvina asks him, scratching him between the ears.

The dog wags its tail, satisfied, and runs off through the trees. He knows they're on their way back.

Edelvina follows him unhurriedly, contemplating how the imminent autumn leaves its traces on nature. Soon the trees that surround the village will turn orange, red and yellow, leaving their branches bare so the winter sun can warm the roofs of the houses.

She smiles. She likes the cyclical character of nature, that internal clock that makes the planet pulse.

Olmo waits for her at the end of the path, giving her a chance to catch up before running off again. He's 6-years-old, but still behaves like a puppy.

'Six years is but a sigh,' whispers Edelvina, brushing away the enormous leaf of a fern.

The light from the lake begins to reflect off the tree trunks as she approaches the gorge, calling to her.

Edelvina knows she still has time for a stop. The Council meeting won't start until twelve, and the sun is still rising up the sky. Olmo understands her intentions immediately and runs back to meet her.

'There's a good dog!' laughs Edelvina, stroking him absent-mindedly as she approaches the knoll.

Moon Rock, as it is called in the village, is a perfect vantage point over the lake. The stone is still cold but, in the afternoon, it will be the favourite meeting point for the younger generation. They will come there to celebrate the last hours of summer and jump into the water, seduced by a short-lived but powerful courage. Warmed by the sunshine, Moon Rock will give off its heat throughout the night.

Edelvina approaches the lip of the rock, the ledge from which she has seen the kids jump. There she looks out over the hollow where her village hides, on the shores of the lake, surrounded by the forest that extends to the peaks of the mountains.

It is hard to make out the green roofs of the houses among the leafy branches of the trees; the walls with their warm hues blend into the landscape. But she knows the street plan of Green Lake perfectly, the free layout of the alleys that run through it. Edelvina knows where to find every detail. She recognises which house is emitting the smoke pouring from the slender chimney.

Olmo stretches out on the rock, allowing her the time she needs. He closes his eyes, trustful. The light reflecting off the lake becomes liquid on Moon Rock. Edelvina looks over the water that is the origin of life. First, she finds the mouth of the stream that crosses the main street of Green Lake, then follows its imaginary trajectory until she finds the gigantic round shadow of the spaceship that fell 50 years ago, its engines mortally wounded.

She knows that the young of the village take bets as to who can reach it every summer. This has happened year after year. They dive, looking for answers, trying to understand why humans were the fathers of their own destruction, wishing that victory had not been achieved upon piles of corpses.

The teacher's explanations are no help, the words of their parents are never enough—young people always need to see, to learn for themselves. That is their strength, but it's also a danger.

'Come on, boy,' says Edelvina, leaving her lookout on the moon rock. 'Time to get a move on.'

They take the wooden path that runs along the wall of the gorge until they reach the upper part of the village, where the last houses are shaded by the forest.

The rhythmic noise of the windmills crowning the orchard roofs like ancient weathervanes sounds to Edelvina like purring, as if the houses were still asleep. But she knows it is not so. She knows that the movement in Green Lake began hours ago, that its inhabitants, like industrious ants, are already blessing the day with their chores. You can smell the freshly baked bread from Servento's house, hear Bal's happy song as she tends to her tomato plants.

Olmo runs off to chase Florina's cat and Edelvina nods, as if that gesture were also part of the perfect choreography of the village.

'Everything is as it should be,' she says. 'As it has always been, as it shall always be.'

She avoids the temptation to complete the sentence: 'If nothing changes…', but she thinks it all the same.

Edelvina corrects herself with a heavy sigh.

She always dreads the late September Councils, and this will be no normal Council. Ten years have passed since the last Awakening.

Today the inhabitants of Green Lake will defend their proposals. They will argue why they consider it necessary to awaken this or that invention from the past. They will discuss progress and its dangers. The doctor will again argue for the ultrasound scanner and the tireless Roberto will insist on the need for television.

'As if we hadn't had enough with the radio,' sighs Edelvina.

She has the hardest task as the representative of Green Lake and will have to act as arbitrator in the discussion, later taking her conclusions to the North Area meeting and, from there, after more arguments, to Winter Equinox.

It all seems so far away now, that moment when, as representative of the Northern Area, she will meet with the other world leaders to take the final decision about which inventions from the past will be reawakened...

Ten years is hardly any time at all between one Awakening and the next. Edelvina fears that progress will speed up again and end up destroying everything they have been building for the last 50 years.

She is not the only one living with that fear, however—many in the village are also against the Awakenings, or at least against their frequency.

'A hundred years!' Gloria always yells when arguments are at their peak. 'A hundred years we should wait between one Awakening and the next!'

Edelvina sometimes feels tempted to agree, but she also knows that 100 years could cause despair to all those who love change, who need to see civilisation advance. Not everyone has a conservative heart like Gloria's.

Her thoughts fly to Fabian Alamo, always so urgent, always desperate to cleanse the memories of the past and create new ones. He is 25 years old, but he already knows that progress is unstoppable, that the global motto of patience and waiting for a gradual recovery is just a prison for the human spirit. Fabian Alamo dreams only of reaching the stars.

And that makes Edelvina doubt. There are days when she doesn't know what's best, when the weight of her job becomes more intense, and she feels like giving up. But she cannot. She has a responsibility.

Her footsteps lead her towards the Council House. It is the only curved-walled building in the village and chamomile flowers continue to grace its great grass-covered dome despite the lateness of the season.

Ten people are already gathered at the door. They chat in groups of 3 or 4, repeating their proposals, checking whether they have their neighbours' support and how reliable their promises are. Throughout September, the most enthusiastic villagers campaign for their inventions.

'The ultrasound scanner will especially help women,' says Mara Tamus with passion as she brandishes two sheets of paper full of tiny symbols.

As soon as she sees her arrive, the doctor turns to her.

'You'll support me, right, Edelvina? As a woman you have to support me,' she insists. 'Pregnancies can be controlled in another way... Before the Final War, ultrasound machines saved lives... Lives!'

'I'm already way beyond conceiving age,' smiles Edelvina. 'But I'm looking forward to hearing your arguments.'

'These ten years have helped me get more data,' says Mara. 'I think I have the winning invention.'

'One of the three inventions,' Gustavo Lengo corrects her hastily. 'All the proposals must be heard. The precision laser, although also used for war, has many advantages for industry and I'm sure they would appreciate it in the Hives.'

Edelvina can't help but frown when she hears about the Hives. She knows that, next year, Lengo's son intends to enter the Hive of Sustained Progress, where engineers and scientists make the most of the inventions that are awakened every 10 years. But she also knows perfectly well how that Hive works. That one causes the most headaches for the heads of the Northern Area. Its research is always at the limit of what is allowed. It is a hotbed of destruction.

Olmo reappears among the gathering villagers and trots up to her, like a faithful guardian, ready to support her unconditionally.

Among the crowd there are other animals running around playing with the children or resting with their owners, taking in the important day with them.

The villagers are dressed in their best clothes. Clean and proud, they know the responsibility they will exercise during the Council. 'The Earth belongs to everyone and to no-one' is a motto that sticks in the minds of the oldest members, while the young gather together, arguing among themselves, longing to reach adulthood so they can also vote at the meeting.

When the bell on the pier strikes a quarter to 12, the villagers enter the Council building and take their seats on the tiers that line the walls.

The discussions reverberate around the dome and Edelvina feels like she is just one more resident. She sees like-minded people grouped together. Fabian Alamo is surrounded by all those who urgently feel the need for progress. They glance cross the circular space, weighing each other up, gauging the situation. And, little by little, while the clock hands move, the voices become murmurs until the most absolute silence receives the chimes again.

Twelve o'clock.

One more year.

'Welcome, inhabitants of Green Lake,' begins Bal Veza, the Council's spokesperson. 'Today, 30 September 2543, we begin the fourth Awakening voting session. Ten proposals have been submitted, but, following tradition, before we listen to their spokespersons, let memory speak.'

Edelvina looks for Gregorio Espino among the townsfolk. The man, bent over with age, gets up slowly and makes his way to the centre of the room. He carries his olive walking stick and wears his wrinkles like medals.

He was a pilot in the Final War. He piloted a B15 like the one that crashed in the woods. He lost his family. But afterwards he scratched the earth with his fingers, cleared the world of mud, and patiently planted the fruits that stand today where before there was only death.

'In 2489, as the last ten hectares of the Amazon reached the maximum level of international protection, the Artificial Intelligence that we all knew as Milae was perfected,' explains Gregorio Espino, using exactly the same words as he did on the 3 previous occasions. 'Four years later, at the same time as the last freshwater reservoir between the tropics disappeared, the representatives of the most powerful governments in the world went to the central base where Milae's great brain operated and asked it this question.'

'What can we do to save the planet?' replied all the villagers in unison.

Edelvina fights back the smile that starts to appear when she sees little 5-year-old Javier stand up solemnly to ask the same question as the grown-ups.

His father immediately pulls him back to his place.

At that very hour, the same ritual will be taking place in all the villages of the North Area. The same ritual that will take place in all the corners of the world throughout those 24 hours. Identical, measured, precise.

Old Gregorio continues.

'Milae did not reply. The Artificial Intelligence fell into a deep silence. It was thinking. And its thoughts told it that, if it shared the answer, it could never really solve the problem that had been put before it.' Gregorio pauses to look at his neighbours.

He always stops at the same point. Right on the border separating the precarious order of humanity and the chaos that the machines would unleash. This is the point when the youngest are most attentive, waiting, hoping, for the story to change, for Milae to speak with a voice full of calm and promise at the last moment.

But that never happens.

The Artificial Intelligence never gives an answer, at least not in the form of words.

'Ten seconds after the world leaders asked their question, the Butler robots working in the houses began the attack,' continues Gregorio Espino, dispassionately. 'At the same time, the Official and Soldier robots received orders from Milae to exterminate humanity, since that was the conclusion the Artificial Intelligence had reached.'

'To save the planet, humanity must be wiped out.' Edelvina anticipates the old man's words. That theory, or similar ones, had been mooted by ecologists since the 20th century, since when they had also tried to control the world population through various means, from legislation to epidemics.

To save the planet, humanity must be wiped out. It is a fallacy, a simplified answer. It is the conclusion of an Artificial Intelligence that humans believed they had perfected, but now could only be seen as primitive. Or, at least, that is what Edelvina Canto resolutely wishes to believe.

That is what Fabian defends every time he is given the chance. 'It's not who, but how,' the boy often repeats. 'It's not how, but when.'

Gregorio continues to describe the battle: massacres in the home, mass exterminations in a matter of seconds, cities destroyed before the armies could organise. In a world that considered the splendour of technology to be the culmination of ascending and sustained progress through the centuries, every space had a robot connected to the Internet and, therefore, to Milae's orders. The Artificial intelligence was the best of generals, the greatest strategist in history.

And the same chaos that was unleashed on Earth devastated the moon and Mars. The ships that tried to return were shot down. Army fighter planes were controlled by systems connected to the network under Milae's control. Resistance was impossible. Technology only obeyed technology.

In a completely digital world, humanity was forced to defend itself with sticks and stones.

'It was only thanks to Lian Wang, who quickly developed an algorithm capable of producing a worldwide electrical blackout, that were we able to save ourselves,' continues the old memory-bearer, nearing the end of his tale. 'Of the more than nine billion people on Earth in the year 2493, only thirty-five million people survived the Final War.'

Edelvina nods, as do many of the villagers.

Yes, Gregorio Espino has again brought back the past for them. Yes, from then on, they will be able to listen to their neighbours' proposals, defend the awakening of harmless inventions, refuse any dangerous technology being brought back.

But the village representative knows that even the most innocent of awakenings can lead to a domino effect, knocking down all the others in a chain of fatal consequences. Humankind must recover part of its scientific and technological heritage, but not at any price, and not at full speed, although that is what the Hives are defending.

Gregorio Espino returns to his seat and his husband pats him gently on the leg, proud of his speech.

Bal Veza clears her throat to speak more clearly.

'Now let us hear the defenders of the Awakening proposals,' she says. 'The first person to speak will be Florinda Sturnus.'

Edelvina smiles. Florinda will defend the industrial steam press, as she does every year. And, just like every year, it will receive a few sympathy votes. Nobody is in favour of the indiscriminate manufacture of paper when there are libraries and you can exchange books with other villages, even if you have to wait weeks. Where is the urgency in that?

Next up, the doctor recounts the advantages of the ultrasound scanner, while Lengo defends the precision laser. And so it goes on, with the mechanical pencil, the motorcycle, the refrigerator, the hunting gun, the recording tape and the thermal fabric presented to the Council. The debate is on.

'We don't need weapons at all,' says one offended neighbour. 'Do you want us to start killing each other again?'

'Weapons create hierarchies,' adds another.

'All your proposals depend on plastic,' points out Gloria. 'The creation of plastic opened the door to decadence.'

'Mechanical pencils can be made from wood and metal,' defends Gema Serardia. 'We wouldn't need to make so many pencils, so could avoid cutting down trees.'

'Pencil manufacturing is totally controlled, for sun's sake,' chimes in a dark-haired boy. 'At this rate we'll end up inventing the wheel.'

Fabian Alamo takes the opportunity to make his speech.

'Does anyone really see any danger in waking up any of these objects?' he asks. 'Do you really think that Laura Manzano has proposed the shotgun so she can get one up on any of you? Have you forgotten the attacks by wolves on the flock of sheep she watches over in winter? What will we do when they kill all our sheep? Wait for our children to be eaten too?'

His questions have captured the Council's attention. The parallel conversations typical of any debate fade away and Fabian takes to his feet. His whole body speaks. His hands accompany each of his questions, his eyes search for the specific gaze of each citizen.

Fabian Alamo is the only one who dares to speak the words that everyone is thinking in the solitude of the room.

'How many awakenings must we wait for to recover the dignity that research and science granted us?' he asks. 'Unlike the rest of our animal brothers, humans enjoy the power of reason. Should we mutilate intellect, paralyse genius? Let's keep picking tomatoes every summer!'

He looks at the gathering. 'Meanwhile, diseases that had been wiped out will attack us again because we couldn't give doctors and biologists the freedom to carry out their research. Plastic made it possible to democratise the use of countless goods, but not only that—it also kept things sterile and allowed practical and effective treatments.'

'And polluted all the seas!' shouts Servento Berro in despair. 'You can still find plastic if you go near the ruins of the old city. Take all you want!'

And the shouting starts up once again under the Council dome.

Edelvina stays out of it. Her role is to listen and wait.

At two in the afternoon, when the pier bell rings and the young ones have left the building to prepare the great celebratory lunch in the square, Bal will call the vote. Then she will write down the results on the sheet of paper for the case and will set off on her journey.

Hunger will be the best ally in voting, and any anger at the results will be quelled by Servento's delicious breads, rich hams, wild strawberries, salads and fresh juices, fish crackling on the coals and apple cider.

Perhaps Fabian will not forget the numbers, perhaps he will insist and ask the neighbours for their votes. He will surely shield himself alongside the young Lengo while they remark how decrepit the generation of their parents and grandparents is. They will dream together of a better future: one over which they will rule.

As long as everything stays in dreams, let no one stop you from dreaming, thinks Edelvina. They wouldn't be young if they didn't aspire to change the planet.

The bell strikes two and the voting begins.

* * *

The journey to the Winter Equinox is a pilgrimage.

A pilgrimage lasting almost 3 months.

Edelvina does the first few kilometres on a speedcycle, driven by the force of the wind and following the route to the sea. She picks up the representatives of all the villages she finds on her way, because Green Lakes is the beginning, and the coast is the end of the route.

With them she comments on the results of the Council's votes. They talk about the danger the speedcycle can pose despite its advantage in speed. They comment on the virtues of the ultrasound scanner and doubt the need to compile everything again on plastic tapes that will require plastic players and end up generating vast amounts of waste.

At the end of October, all the representatives board a ship that takes them up the coast to the capital of the Northern Area, next to the Hive of Sustained Progress. It takes them 10 days to get there, leaving enough time to rest until 16 November, the date of the General Council.

Voting at the North Area meeting is much easier and faster. There, debate is kept to a minimum. The proposals are assessed on the basis of 3 parameters: immediate usefulness in improving human life; waste generation in manufacture and recycling; and potential for chaos. Because, as Edelvina knows, each step on the path of progress opens countless doors to total destruction. Electricity may seem magical when you turn on a light bulb in the dark, but it was also what fed Milae.

The representatives of all the villages in the Northern Area easily reach an agreement. Edelvina will take her 3 proposals to the Winter Equinox meeting, since she is the longest-serving village representative. There she will defend the awakening of the polypropylene prosthesis, the Cloud ship and the electric harvester.

On 17 November, Edelvina boards an airship able to cross the Pacific Ocean. She lands in Free Port on 18 November and, from there, she travels again by speedcycle for 30 days to the north, visiting countless villages on her way and checking that order and peace continue to prevail on Earth.

Her journey is always accompanied by the hospitality and generosity of everyone she meets. She always finds a warm bed to sleep in and a friendly offer of a bathroom to wash in.

On 18 November at 10 o'clock at night, Edelvina arrives at Winter Equinox, the only settlement on the entire planet with a population of more than 500 people.

* * *

High-rise buildings have always brought back bad memories for Edelvina. She understands that in a city of 2,000 inhabitants it is more logical to build upwards than to destroy the landscape with countless houses. But still, Winter Equinox looks too much like the past. No matter how the vines grow, trying to hide the steel and cement, or how lush and extensive the parks are... The noise of the speedcycles can be heard in the avenues connecting the main buildings, and the citizens move with an urgency she finds artificial after so many years in High Lake.

For the first time, she misses Olmo. Stroking her dog's head now would have made things easier.

Slowly, decisively, Edelvina heads along the stone pavement towards the Awakening building.

It is built in a style that imitates the Council Houses in the villages. Like them it's circular and is topped with a green dome that will look much nicer once spring arrives and it becomes covered with flowers. But it's bigger, so very much bigger. Because once a year it houses the 2,000 inhabitants of the city.

Edelvina knows it is a necessary evil. She understands that managing a planet needs many heads, and that each of the inhabitants of Winter Equinox fulfils a specific function. And yet, she pities the artificial existence its citizens are forced to endure. They move to rhythms marked not by the sun but by their obligations. Their shifts overlap so that they can respond by radio to a humankind that wakes up at different times of the day, depending on the latitude of the villages.

That very precision, that permanent state of alert, contains the seeds of failure. Because urgency generates unhappiness and, when they feel sad, humans seek solutions and exercise their creativity. That is why no-one may live more than 5 years in Winter Equinox. Once they have provided their services, they must return to their village.

'Identify yourself,' asks a young woman, stationed at the front door of the Awakening building.

'Edelvina Canto, from Green Lake, representative of the North Area,' she replies, putting on her friendliest smile.

The woman checks the list on her sheet and nods her through.

Edelvina thanks her profusely but receives no response. This is what the city does to you, she thinks, a village-dweller through and through.

She follows the hallway until she reaches the door that leads to the large meeting room. There will be only 53 representatives and the tiers of seats will look like a ridiculous mockery, but such is tradition.

A young man is waiting for her there and offers her a glass bottle of water and a glass.

'For a green kingdom,' he tells her with a smile.

'For a green kingdom,' replies Edelvina, thinking it must be his first year in the city.

The youth opens the door for her and closes it behind her as she enters the circular room.

Edelvina smiles broadly as she recognises her companions. Everyone takes their place in silence. They are sitting in perfect symmetry on the seats in exactly the same positions as the three previous Awakenings.

She walks calmly to her seat and places the bottle and glass on the small adjacent table. She will only have to wait 10 minutes; everything in the Awakening building also follows a systematic ritual. After her, the representative of the South Area will file in. And lastly, the representatives of the Cordillera Area and the East Area will appear together.

Everything is according to the rules.

Everything happens just as it should.

When the bell of the World Communications Centre strikes 12 in the distance, Eva Sneg, the spokesperson for the Awakening announces:

'Today, 21 December 2543, we begin the fourth voting session of the Awakening. Representatives, you may send your annual reports.'

Edelvina goes into her file system and compresses the information she has received from the representatives of all the villages in the North Area. In a blink, she launches the data to the main memory.

The information intersects instantly with that provided by the other representatives. At top speed, the central memory looks for any detail that could set off any alarm bells, leading to possible drastic decisions.

'Now send the repair and maintenance logs,' orders Eva Sneg.

The silence in the circular room is total. The representatives work with the maximum efficiency.

'Sending Awakening decisions, territory changes, and responses to individual requests,' says Eva. 'Androids, you may go into hibernation mode while the system update is in progress.'

Edelvina placidly closes her eyes. Everything is fine. The planet is still in order. Milae's will prevails.

This is the time of year when she is most at peace.

About the Authors

Aleksandra (Ola) Hill is a Polish-Canadian writer and the founder and editor-in-chief of khōréō, a quarterly magazine of speculative fiction by immigrant and diaspora writers. Her stories have previously won the grand prize in the 2019 Writer's Digest Popular Fiction Contest, been shortlisted for the 2021 Uncharted Magazine Summer Sci-Fi/Fantasy Short Story Award, and received an honourable mention in the 2021 CRAFT Short Fiction Prize. You can find her slinking around NYC bookstores and on Twitter at @_aleksandrahill.

Andrew Darlington watched the very first episode of 'Dr Who', he also watched the most recent episode. Whatever academic potential he may once have possessed was wrecked by an addiction to loud Rock 'n' Roll and cheap Science Fiction, which remain the twin poles of what he laughingly refers to as his writing career. He is most proud of his Parallel Universe fiction collection 'A Saucerful Of Secrets'. His latest books include a biography of the Beatles spin-doctor 'Derek Taylor: For Your Radioactive Children', and 'On Track: The Hollies, Every Album, Every Song' (both from SonicBond Books). His writing can be found at 'Eight Miles Higher': http://andrewdarlington.blogspot.co.uk.

Caroline Misner's work has appeared in publications throughout the USA, Canada, India and the UK. She has been nominated for numerous awards, including the Governor Generals Award in 2018 for her novel "The Spoon Asylum". She lives in the beautiful Haliburton Highlands of Northern Ontario, Canada, where she continues to draw inspiration for her work. You can view more of her work at her website: http://carolinemisner.com.

Chinaza Eziaghighala is a medical doctor who tells stories. An interdisciplinary writer at the intersection of health, film, comics and literature, she is a University of Iowa International Writing

Program Alum. Her works are in/forthcoming British Science Fiction Association's Fission, Metastellar, African Writer, Brittle Paper, Afritondo and British Science Fiction Association's Focus. CHIMERA, her debut novella, is forthcoming in 2024 from Nosetouch Press. She is a member of the Science Fiction Writers Association of America, a First Reader for Cosmic Roots and Eldritch Shores and a Guest Nonfiction Editor for Please See Me. Connect with her here: http://chinazaeziaghighala.disha.page or @chinazaezims on Twitter.

Clare Turner is a private tutor of maths, physics, and astronomy, based in Manchester. She left the world of aerospace engineering research to teach, write, and be her own boss. She is a strong advocate for women in STEM and works to share her love of maths and science with everyone. She currently has a hard science fiction novel under development, but also enjoys writing flash fiction in several genres. Outside of science fact and fiction, Clare's loves are hiking, scrambling, and her husband.

David Tallerman is the author of numerous books: the historical science-fiction drama *To End All Wars,* thrillers *A Savage Generation* and *The Bad Neighbour,* fantasy series *The Black River Chronicles* and *The Tales of Easie Damasco,* and the science-fiction novella *Patchwerk.* His most recent release is *The Outfit,* an account of the true-life Tiflis Bank Robbery and the part played in it by future leader of the Soviet Union Joseph Stalin. His short fiction has appeared in over a hundred markets, among them Clarkesworld, Nightmare, Lightspeed, and Beneath Ceaseless Skies. He can be found online at http://www.davidtallerman.co.uk.

Ellen Denton is a freelance writer living in the Rocky Mountains with her husband and two demonic cats who wreak havoc and hell (the cats, not the husband). Her writing has been published in over a hundred magazines and anthologies. She, as well, has had an exciting life working as a circus clown, a Navy seal, and an exotic dancer in the crew lounge of the starship Enterprise. *(Writer's note: The one-hundred-plus publication credits are true, but some or all of the other stuff may be fictional.*)

Eugen Bacon is an African Australian author of several novels and fiction collections. Her recent books *Ivory's Story, Danged Black Thing* and *Saving Shadows* are finalists in the BSFA Awards. Eugen was announced in the honor list of the 2022 Otherwise Fellowships for 'doing exciting work in gender and speculative fiction'. She has won, been longlisted or commended in international awards, including the Aurealis Award, Foreword Indies, Bridport Prize, Copyright Agency Prize, Horror Writers Association Diversity Grant, Otherwise, Rhysling, Australian Shadows, Ditmar Awards and Nommo Awards for Speculative Fiction by Africans.
Visit her website at http://eugenbacon.com and Twitter feed **@EugenBacon**

Gene Rowe is a cognitive psychologist by profession. He has written many *supposedly* worthy academic articles and book chapters, reviewed countless more for over 50 different journals, and had extensive editorial experience. However, he far prefers the realm of fiction. His first novel (*The Greater Game,* White Cat Publications) has at last been published (2022), and he is close to finalising two more – a vast sci-fi/fantasy hybrid, and a comic sci-fi novel set in Norwich, where he lives and works. Watch this space?

Ian Whates is the author of ten published novels (two co-written), two novellas, and some eighty short stories that have appeared in a variety of venues, including *Nightmare Magazine, Galaxy's Edge, Daily Science Fiction,* and the science journal *Nature.* In 2019 he received the Karl Edward Wagner Award from the British Fantasy Society, while his work has been shortlisted for the Philip K. Dick Award and on three occasions for BSFA Awards. He is the editor of more than 40 anthologies as well as editing PS Publishing's *ParSec* magazine. In 2006 Ian accidentally founded award-winning independent publisher NewCon Press.

Jeff Somers (http://www.jeffreysomers.com) began writing by court order as an attempt to steer his creative impulses away from engineering genetic grotesqueries. He has published nine novels, including the Avery Cates series the Ustari Cycle series, as well as over fifty short stories, including "Ringing the Changes," which was selected for inclusion in *Best American Mystery Stories 2006.* He is a contributing editor at *Writer's Digest Magazine*, which also published his book on the craft of writing *Writing Without Rules*. He lives in Hoboken with his wife, The Duchess, and their cats. He considers pants to always be optional.

KC Grifant is a Southern Californian author who writes internationally published horror, fantasy, science fiction and weird west stories for podcasts, anthologies and magazines. Her writings have appeared in Andromeda Spaceways Magazine, Unnerving Magazine, Cosmic Horror Monthly, Tales to Terrify, the Lovecraft eZine, and many others. She's also contributed to dozens of anthologies, including: Chromophobia; Field Notes from a Nightmare; The One That Got Away; Six Guns Straight From Hell; Shadowy Natures; Beyond the Infinite: Tales from the Outer Reaches; and the Stoker-nominated Fright Mare: Women Write Horror. A co-founder of the San Diego HWA chapter, she enjoys chasing a wild toddler and wandering through beachside carnivals. For details, visit http://www.KCGrifant.com or @kcgrifant.

Maddison Stoff is a neurodiverse non-binary writer from Melbourne, Australia. She writes a combination of experimental and pulp-inspired science fiction set in a continuous universe. Her fiction has appeared in *Aurealis* and *Andromeda Spaceways Magazine*, her essays in *Overland*, and her short story collection *For We Are Young and Free* is out now on Dostoyevsky Wannabe. She also has an auto-biographical mini-comic called *Machine Translations: A Robot's Path to Self-Expression and Learning to Live With Organics*. Follow her on Twitter and Patreon @thedescenters.

Mary Soon Lee was born and raised in London but has lived in Pittsburgh for over twenty years. Her latest books are from opposite ends of the poetry spectrum: "Elemental Haiku," containing haiku for the periodic table, and "The Sign of the Dragon," an epic fantasy with Chinese elements, winner of the 2021 Elgin Award. She hides her online presence with a cryptically named website (marysoonlee.com) and an equally cryptic Twitter account (@MarySoonLee).

Michael Noonan lives in Halifax, England, has a background in food production, retail and office work. Has had stories published in the anthology volumes *Even More Tonto Stories* and *Shades of Sentience*. Has had a volume of short stories published, entitled *Seven Tall Tales* that is available on Amazon, as a book or a kindle. His play, *The Town That Spoke with Forked Tongue,* has been accepted by the internet publisher, Scripts For Stage, and a comic one act play, entitled, *Elvis and The Psychiatrist,* has been shown at the Snowdance Comedy Festival at the Sixth Theatre in Racine Wisconsin.

Patricia Gacía-Rojo (Jaén, 1984) teaches Literature and Spanish Language and also writes poetry and narrative for children and young adults. After winning the 'Andalucía Joven' Narrative Award in 2008, she began publishing and since then she hasn´t stopped. She has won the 'Gran Angular' award with 'El mar' (SM, 2015), the 'Hache' award with 'Lobo. El camino de la venganza' (SM, 2016), the 'Ciudad de Málaga' award with 'El secreto de Olga' (Anaya, 2019) and the 'Templis' and 'Kelvin' awards with 'El asesino de Alfas' (SM, 2021). To this day, she has more than twenty published novels.

Peter Medeiros teaches writing at Emerson College and the Boston non-profit GrubStreet, and Kung Fu at Davis Square Martial Arts. His work has appeared in over a dozen publications, most recently in *Swords and Sorcery Magazine* and *The Worlds Within*. He is particularly interested in SFF that explores issues of education and community. He is represented by Susan Valezquez at JABerwocky Literary Agency.

Phil Nicholls is the in-house feature writer at Proactive Publications, husband, father to two boys, table-top gamer and butler to three contrary cats. He lives in Norfolk, England, in a house filled with books, games and laughter. For thirty years he has told tall tales in many forms. In 2020 he joined the BSFA and a friendly Orbiter writing group. He currently reviews books for

Shoreline of Infinity and BSFA Review. He also writes SF shorts and children's stories. For NaNoWriMo21 Phil began working on his first SF novel.

Ron Hardwick was born in Wallsend-on-Tyne but now resides in East Lothian, Scotland. He is married with one son and a grandson. He has Master of Arts degrees in both Literature and Creative Writing from the University That Never Sleeps, and especially enjoys writing science fantasy narratives. He has self-published four volumes of short stories on Amazon Kindle and has had other work published by e-zines such as *Secret Attic, Makarelle, Write Time* and *Cranked Anvil.* He has 28 short stories of his fictional comic private eye Mr Lemon awaiting a publisher!

Tim O'Neal writes shorts stories to pass the long hours of intergalactic travel. His diverse fiction has appeared in electronic publications across the US, UK, and Canada. His story 'Face Thieves' won first prize in *Page Turner Magazine* and his story 'Last Dragonride' featured in the Earth-based *Ember Literary Journal.* As a trained professional in dietetics and exercise, Tim loves to stay active, but aside from time spent in the delicate art of spaceship maintenance, he's discovered the vacuum of the universe makes getting outside rather difficult.

Printed in Great Britain
by Amazon